"You Have The Right To Remain Silent," Seth Said Sensually.

He moved his hands down Hannah's arms and circled her wrists with his fingers as if he'd handcuffed her. "If you give up that right," he continued, "then anything you say can and will be used against you." He lifted her arms over her head and gently pinned her to the sofa beneath him.

His lips touched hers; he nipped at the corner of her mouth, then her bottom lip. His lips teased endlessly. Sensation after sensation shimmered through her, each one more exquisite than the one before.

Impossible, she thought dimly. This is simply not happening. She was certain that she would wake from this erotic dream any second. Only, she didn't want to.

She wanted to know, wanted to *feel* what would happen next....

Dear Reader,

What could be more satisfying than the sinful yet guilt-free pleasure of enjoying six new passionate, powerful and provocative Silhouette Desire romances this month?

Get started with *In Blackhawk's Bed*, July's MAN OF THE MONTH and the latest title in the SECRETS! miniseries by Barbara McCauley. *The Royal & the Runaway Bride* by Kathryn Jensen—in which the heroine masquerades as a horse trainer and becomes a princess—is the seventh exciting installment in DYNASTIES: THE CONNELLYS, about an American family that discovers its royal roots.

A single mom melts the steely defenses of a brooding ranch hand in *Cowboy's Special Woman* by Sara Orwig, while a detective with a secret falls for an innocent beauty in *The Secret Millionaire* by Ryanne Corey. A CEO persuades a mail-room employee to be his temporary wife in the debut novel *Cinderella & the Playboy* by Laura Wright, praised by *New York Times* bestselling author Debbie Macomber as "a wonderful new voice in Silhouette Desire." And in *Zane: The Wild One* by Bronwyn Jameson, the mayor's daughter turns up the heat on the small town's bad boy made good.

So pamper the romantic in you by reading all six of these great new love stories from Silhouette Desire!

Enjoy!

Joan Marlow Golan

Joan Marlow Golan
Senior Editor, Silhouette Desire

Please address questions and book requests to:
Silhouette Reader Service
U.S.: 3010 Walden Ave., P.O. Box 1325, Buffalo, NY 14269
Canadian: P.O. Box 609, Fort Erie, Ont. L2A 5X3

In Blackhawk's Bed
BARBARA McCAULEY

Silhouette® Desire®

Published by Silhouette Books
America's Publisher of Contemporary Romance

SILHOUETTE BOOKS

ISBN 0-373-76447-2

IN BLACKHAWK'S BED

This edition published by arrangement with Harlequin Books S.A.

® and TM are trademarks of Harlequin Books S.A., used under license. Trademarks indicated with ® are registered in the United States Patent and Trademark Office, the Canadian Trade Marks Office and in other countries.

Visit Silhouette at www.eHarlequin.com

Printed in U.S.A.

Books by Barbara McCauley

*Hearts of Stone
†Secrets!

BARBARA McCAULEY,

who has written more than twenty novels for Silhouette Books, lives in Southern California with her own handsome hero husband, Frank, who makes it easy to believe in and write about the magic of romance. Barbara's stories have won and been nominated for numerous awards, including the prestigious RITA® Award from the Romance Writers of America, Best Desire of the Year from *Romantic Times* and Best Short Contemporary from the National Reader's Choice Awards.

One

WELCOME TO RIDGEWATER, TEXAS. POPULA-
TION 3,546. HOME OF THE WORLD'S LARGEST
FRUITCAKE!

Seth Granger stared at the twenty-foot billboard de-
picting a smiling family of four standing beside a God-
zilla-sized fruitcake with bright red cherries on top.

Fruitcake?

After eight years as an Albuquerque undercover cop,
Seth thought he'd seen it all. He stared up at the towering depiction of fruits and nuts.

Apparently, he hadn't.

Shaking his head, he downshifted, then slowed his
Harley to the respectable speed of twenty-five. The last
thing he needed was a ticket in this one-fruitcake town.
After six hours on the West Texas highway in the blis-

tering late-summer sun, what Seth needed was a full tank of gas, the biggest, juiciest cheeseburger he could find and a great big glass of ice water. By tonight, he'd be in Sweetwater where he could find a motel, then the closest bar. He'd been itching for an icy mug of Corona all day, and he could already taste the crisp, amber brew sliding down his dust-dry throat.

Throw in a pepperoni pizza, a pretty waitress, and that was about as perfect as life got.

A middle-aged woman walking a little black terrier on the side of the highway stared at him as he approached. The dog yapped and tugged on its leash, then circled the woman's legs, nearly tripping her. Seth glanced at her as he passed. The woman glared back.

So much for small-town hospitality, he thought.

But even he had to admit he was looking a little scruffy. He hadn't shaved in a couple of days and his thick black hair was almost to his shoulders. He'd had to let it grow for his last assignment—infiltrating a meth-lab operation—and he hadn't cut it yet. Top that off with a motorcycle and a pair of aviator glasses, and he looked like the front cover of *Bad Ass Bikers*.

The late-afternoon heat rippled in waves off the asphalt as he turned into the gas station and drew stares from the people gassing their cars. He rumbled to a stop in front of a pump and pulled his helmet off. While he filled his tank, Seth scanned the station. Everyone quickly looked away.

He wondered what the good people of Ridgewater would do if he yelled ''Boo!'' and started waving his arms around. Jump in their cars, most likely, and peel out of the station as if Satan himself was on their tail. The thought made him smile.

But he resisted the temptation to follow through. He

had more pressing, important things to give brain space to than what the people of Ridgewater thought of him.

Like the letter in his backpack from Beddingham, Barnes and Stephens's law office.

There'd been a mound of mail when Seth had finally come home after the fiasco of his last assignment. He hadn't intended to read any of the tower of bills or advertising brochures that night. All he'd wanted was an ice pack for his aching hand and a bottle of José Cuervo.

But the letter had been on top of the pile, all those lawyers' names staring at him like a neon sign, and Seth had picked it up. No doubt someone intended to sue him. Maybe a disgruntled drug dealer who hadn't appreciated being arrested, Seth figured, or maybe that bastard in apartment 12-C who liked to beat up his wife had resented Seth's interference a few weeks earlier. Jeez, the list could have gone on forever, he supposed and he'd dropped the letter back on the pile.

But as he'd filled a bag with ice, then poured himself a shot of tequila, he'd come back to the letter. That's when he'd noticed the return address was Wolf River County, Texas.

He froze.

Wolf River?

He'd tossed back the drink in his hand, then reached for the envelope and ripped it open.

And now, standing here in this Ridgewater, Texas, gas station, Seth remembered every word of that letter. But no words more clearly than the second paragraph, third line…

…Rand Zacharias Blackhawk and Elizabeth Marie Blackhawk, son and daughter of Jonathan and No-

rah Blackhawk of Wolf River County, Texas, were
not killed in the car accident that claimed the lives
of their parents…

There'd been more, of course. The name of the lawyer to call at the office, a phone number, something
about an estate, though from what little Seth remembered of his childhood, the small ranch his parents had
owned certainly couldn't have been worth much.

But Seth didn't give a damn about that, anyway. All
he could think about was the fact that Rand and Lizzie
hadn't died.

That they were alive.

Alive.

His first thought was that it was a mistake, a *huge*
mistake. Or even worse, some kind of sick joke. But no
one knew anything about his past. No one knew that
for the first seven years of his life, until he'd been
adopted by Ben and Susan Granger, Seth's last name
had been Blackhawk. Seth himself barely remembered.

Seth stared at the numbers flashing by on the gas
pump. He'd only been seven then. Rand, his older
brother, had been nine. Elizabeth—Lizzie, they'd all
called her—she'd just turned two.

The letter had felt like a two-by-four slamming
against his chest. The air had literally been sucked from
his lungs. To find out, after twenty-three years, that the
brother and sister he'd thought had died were still alive,
was absolutely and completely staggering.

He couldn't remember how long he'd sat there in the
dark, on the edge of the sofa in his apartment, and stared
at that letter. But when the light had begun to seep
through the dusty blinds in his living room, Seth had
finally dialed the lawyer's office and left a message.

Then he'd sat back down, with the phone in his lap, and waited.

It was true. The lawyer confirmed it when he'd finally called back. Rand and Lizzie hadn't died. Rand had been found, but they were still looking for Lizzie, somewhere back east, or in the south.

Can he come to Wolf River? the lawyer had asked.

Could he come?

Hell, yes, he'd come, Seth had told the lawyer.

His heart racing, his hand shaking, Seth had hung up the phone, still sat there staring at the receiver for a full fifteen minutes. After that, he'd slept for the next sixteen hours straight.

The fact that he'd been suspended from the force for six weeks had made it easy to throw a few clothes and necessities into a bag and head out. It wasn't as if he had anything to keep him in Albuquerque. No wife. No kids. No commitments.

Which was exactly the way he'd wanted it. He'd tried living with Julie, his last girlfriend, but the life of an undercover cop was hardly what anyone would consider a stable relationship. He never knew when he'd be home, or even *if* he'd be home. He'd warned Julie about his lifestyle, but she'd sworn she understood and could adjust to his erratic schedules.

So she'd cheerfully moved in, adding those little feminine touches around the apartment: sunflower coasters, a hand-knitted throw on the sofa, scented candles in the bathroom. Framed photos of the two of them everywhere.

But after six months, with more than half that time spent alone, Julie's understanding had been stretched like a rubber band. When she finally snapped, she'd moved out in a dramatic display—a ritualistic burning of every photo of the two of them together, the pictures all tossed into a metal trash can that she'd placed in the middle of his living room. For good measure she'd thrown in the knitted throw, too, which had created so much smoke the fire department had shown up, along with a patrol car.

For weeks after that, he'd been the brunt of countless jokes at the station. A key chain fire extinguisher, smoke detectors, a fireman's hat.

No more live-ins, he'd firmly decided after all that. He didn't want that kind of complication in his life, and he wasn't so foolish as not to know that once a woman invaded a man's space, she immediately started thinking rings and weddings and babies. All those things were fine for a nine-to-five kind of guy, but he simply didn't fit that profile.

He'd seen the agony on his adopted mother's face the night his father's best friends from the force had knocked on the front door, their faces solemn and heads bowed. Al Mott and Bob Davis had been Uncle Al and Uncle Bob to Seth for the past ten years. After the funeral, they'd both told Seth not to join the department. Go to college and be an accountant or an architect, they'd said. Seth's mother cried the day he'd joined the Albuquerque Police Department, but she'd hugged him and given her blessing.

That had been ten years ago. Two years as a rookie, then straight to undercover. There were days, too many of late, that Seth thought Al and Bob had been right. Pushing a pencil and sitting in a cushy office chair was sounding more appealing all the time.

Especially after this last job, he thought with a sigh.

When the gas pump clicked off, Seth topped the Harley's tank with another shot from the nozzle, tugged his helmet back on, then climbed back on his motorcycle. At the pump on the other side of the island, a gray-haired woman filling her white Taurus with gas stared at him. Seth slipped his sunglasses down and winked at her. Appalled, the woman quickly turned away.

Smiling to himself, Seth roared out of the gas station, knowing full well that every eye in the place was watching him leave.

He'd be out of this town and back on the road within the hour, he told himself. If he was lucky, sooner.

Tall elm trees and old Victorian homes lined the main road into town. Several of the houses had business signs out front: an antique shop, a law office, a doctor. On the lower left corner of every sign was the painted picture of a fruitcake. Seth shook his head at the absurdity of it, thankful he didn't live here. He couldn't imagine telling people he was from the land of giant fruitcakes.

Correction, fruit*cake*.

He was nearly at the end of the shady street when he spotted a child inside the white picket fence surrounding the large front yard of one of the homes. The child, a little girl with shiny blond curls, stood under an elm tree, waving her arms frantically. Seth slowed his motorcycle, then felt his heart stop at the sight of another little girl in the tree, dangling in midair ten feet off the ground, her bright blue pants obviously caught on the branch. A look of sheer terror on her face, the child's eyes were squeezed tightly closed.

There were times when a person didn't think, they simply acted.

Seth jumped the curb and crashed through the picket fence. His bike went down on the wet grass as he leapt off, yanking his helmet off as he rushed the tree, then scrambled up the main trunk to the branch where the little girl still held on.

"Hang on, honey," Seth yelled to the youngster.

Eyes wide, the child turned her head toward him as he climbed out on the tree branch. The little girl dropped down another three inches as her pants ripped.

Dammit, dammit, dammit!

"Be still," Seth told the child. "Don't even breathe."

The child obeyed, but kept her eyes on him as he made his way across the branch.

"Maddie!"

Seth ignored the sound of a woman's scream from the ground below. Inching his way out toward the child, he reached down and grabbed her by her waist.

"I've got you," Seth reassured the child as he yanked her up. The woman who'd screamed, a blonde with a mass of wild curls on top of her head, stood in the V of the tree trunk, her arms outstretched as she reached for the child. Seth sat on the branch, then handed the little girl over to the woman.

"Mommy!" the child threw her arms around her mother's neck.

Seth let loose the breath he'd been holding. That had been close, he thought with a sigh of relief. Too close. That little girl could have been seriously—

The branch underneath him cracked loudly.

Uh-oh.

Seth did his best to scramble backward, but the branch cracked again and went down, taking him along. The ground rushed up to meet him and everything went black.

Hannah Michaels watched in horror as the man and the tree branch crashed and fell to the ground. With

Maddie still clutching her neck, Hannah slid down the tree trunk and rushed to kneel beside the unconscious man. He lay on his back, absolutely still, his long legs sprawled, his arms spread wide. She wasn't even certain he was breathing.

Oh dear Lord, Hannah thought frantically. They'd killed him.

She pressed a hand to his chest, felt the heavy thud of his heart. A wave of relief washed over her. Thank God. She closed her eyes and sucked in a breath. He was alive.

"Madeline Nicole," Hannah said sternly as she unwrapped her daughter's arms from her neck. "You stand beside your sister and don't move one inch. Do you understand me?"

Lip quivering, Maddie joined Missy, who stood several feet away, her eyes wide and fearful. The twins clasped hands and leaned into each other.

"Hannah Michaels, what in tarnation is going on over there?" Mrs. Peterson, Hannah's next-door neighbor called out from her front porch. "Is that a motorcycle on your front lawn?"

"Could you please call Dr. Lansky over here?" Hannah said over her shoulder. "Tell him it's an emergency."

"An emergency?" Mrs. Peterson craned her neck. "What kind of emergency?"

"Please, Mrs. Peterson," Hannah said more firmly. "Someone's been hurt."

"Hurt? Dear me, I better call right away then. Though it is Tuesday. He might be at the clinic, or he might have taken that grandson of his fishing over at Brightman Lake. He does that sometimes and—"

"Mrs. Peterson, *please.*"

"Oh, yes, dear. Of course, I'll ring him right away." The elderly woman spun on her orthopedic heels and hurried back into her house.

Hannah touched the man's cheek, thankful that it was warm and not cold or clammy. His long, black hair fell over half his face and Hannah gently brushed it aside with her fingers. His features were sculpted, a rugged display of sharp, masculine angles that suggested to Hannah a native American heritage. A gash over his left eye oozed blood, and a lump was already swelling on his forehead. He moaned again.

"Lie still," she whispered. "The doctor will be here in a minute."

He answered her with another moan. His heavy eyelids fluttered, but did not open. Hannah ran her hands carefully over his shoulders, was amazed at the rock-hard feel of muscles under her fingers. His black T-shirt was torn from the collar to the arm, but she didn't see any wounds there other than a deep scratch. She continued her exploration down his arms, praying she wouldn't find anything broken. He seemed just as solid everywhere her hands moved: his chest, his thighs, his legs. Though every ounce of the man appeared to be solid muscle and he certainly appeared fit and in shape, she realized that didn't mean he didn't have internal injuries, a concussion or broken bones.

Moving back up to his face, Hannah winced at the sight of the nasty gash over his eye. She could only imagine the headache this man was going to have when he did finally wake up.

She reached into the pocket of her jeans for a tissue, realized she'd already used it earlier to wipe grape jelly off Maddie's face. She glanced down at the pink T-shirt she had on, then took hold of the hem and leaned over the man to dab at the trail of blood sliding down his face.

Who was he? she wondered. Hannah had been born in this town and had lived here twenty-six years. She knew just about everyone in Ridgewater and the surrounding areas, but she'd never seen this man before. She glanced at his motorcycle, lying on its side in the corner of her yard. New Mexico license plates. Just another biker passing through, she supposed.

Hannah still wasn't certain what had happened. Just a few moments ago, Missy and Maddie had been playing with their dolls on the living-room floor while Hannah had been arguing on the phone with Aunt Martha, the same argument she and her aunt had been having for the past two years.

"It's not proper, Hannah Louise," her aunt said every time they spoke. "A single woman raising two little girls in a backwoods Texas town. They need culture and family and a respectable upbringing." And the demand that Hannah hated the most: "You absolutely must give up your ridiculous idea of a bed and breakfast. We'll sell the house, then you and the girls can come live with me in Boston."

No matter how many times Hannah had told her aunt that she and the girls were happy living in Ridgewater, in the house that had belonged first to her grandparents, then her parents, and now Aunt Martha and herself, Hannah couldn't seem to make the woman understand. To make matters worse, after hearing the crash and Missy's cry, Hannah had hung up the phone on her aunt.

But she'd worry about Aunt Martha later, Hannah told herself. At the moment, she had a more pressing, more important matter to deal with in the form of a very tall, two-hundred-pound-plus unconscious biker.

The man moved his head from side to side and groaned again. Hannah laid a hand on his arm and leaned closer. "Try not to move," she said softly.

His eyes sprang open. Hannah opened her mouth to say something, but before anything could come out, the man sat abruptly, an expression of fierce anger on his face as he grabbed her roughly by the arms.

"Where's Vinnie?" he demanded.

"Vinnie?"

"He was behind me, dammit," the man demanded. "Where the hell is he?"

"I—I don't know who—"

"We're under fire, dammit," he yelled at her. "Tell Jarris to hold back."

Hannah placed her palms on the man's chest and attempted to ease him back down on the grass, but she might as well have had her hands on a brick wall. His fingers dug painfully into her arms.

"I'll tell Jarris." She softened her voice. "You just lie back."

He stared at her with dark, narrowed eyes, but Hannah knew that he really didn't see her. Wherever he was at the moment, it was far away from here. And it certainly wasn't a pleasant place, either.

He blinked at her, and Hannah watched the haze clear in his eyes. "What the—" He looked down where her hands were planted firmly on his chest, then back up at her. "Who are you?"

"Hannah Michaels," she said evenly, though her heart was pounding furiously in her chest. "Now would you please be still until the doctor gets here?"

She pushed on his chest again, gently, but he didn't budge. "Please."

He hesitated, then finally his grip loosened and his shoulders relaxed. He lay back on the grass, then suddenly came up again, winced at the effort. "The kid— up in the tree. Is she—"

"She's fine." Hannah held pressure on his chest until he was flat on the ground again. "Thanks to you, she is."

This man, however, was not quite so lucky. Hannah noted the growing lump on his forehead, the blood and scratches, and felt her stomach clench.

"My bike." He lifted his head to stare at the Harley. That's when he started to swear.

"Maddie and Missy." Hannah glanced at her wide-eyed daughters. They'd never heard such colorful expressions before. "In the house, on the sofa, right now."

Still holding hands, the girls backed toward the house, then turned and ran up the steps. When the screen door slammed behind them, Hannah had to swallow the emotion rising in her. She didn't want to think about what would have happened if this stranger hadn't come along when he had. What she needed to focus on was that Maddie was fine, and the man who'd saved her needed attention.

"I'm sorry about your bike," Hannah said. "I'll cover any expenses for repairs, plus medical bills and any other costs incurred to you."

Of course, she had no idea *how* she would do that, but she'd deal with that later.

"Forget about it." He started to rise again, then swayed slightly. "I'll be fine."

"You're not fine," Hannah insisted. "Now lie back down."

Seth didn't want to lie back down. He wanted to get on his bike and get the hell out of this town before any more disasters befell him. But he wasn't so stupid as not to realize that it was his head spinning, not the ground underneath him.

Dammit, anyway.

He just needed a minute, that was all, he told himself. Maybe two or three, before his equilibrium settled back down again.

He looked at the woman kneeling beside him. She was slender, with a wild mass of blond curls tumbling around her porcelain-smooth, heart-shaped face. Her eyes were as big and blue as the sky overhead, her lashes thick and dark.

His gaze dropped to her mouth. Wide, curved at the corners, inviting.

Damn.

Then his gaze dropped lower, over the pink T-shirt she wore and he saw the blood. He frowned. "Is that mine?"

She glanced down. "Your head is bleeding. You really shouldn't move until the doctor gets here."

"I don't need a doctor." He attempted to stand, hesitated when the ground tilted, then pushed himself up onto his feet.

And immediately felt his legs buckle.

The woman's arms circled him, steadied him even as the world around him swirled. He had to hold on or bring both of them down. He wrapped his arms around her, blinked several times and sucked in a breath at the rocket of pain shooting up his left leg.

"That's gotta hurt," the woman—Hannah—said impatiently. "Now are you going to lie back down, or do I have to get tough?"

If his leg weren't hurting so badly, Seth might have laughed at Hannah's threat. Since she weighed nearly half what he did and was probably six or seven inches shorter than him, he couldn't imagine this woman getting tough.

But as she held him close against her, as the feel of her soft breasts pressed against his chest registered through the haze of pain, Seth began to imagine other things. His body responded to her closeness and the faint scent of her floral perfume. Though he was certain he didn't need her assistance, he let her hold him for a moment, let himself enjoy her arms circling his chest and the feel of her slender curves pressed against him. He might be injured, but he certainly wasn't dead.

"I really think you should lie down now," she persisted.

In a different scenario, one where they were both naked, those words would have been music to his ears and he would have readily agreed. In this case, unfortunately, he simply wanted to gain his balance back and get the hell out of town.

He stepped away from the woman, wobbled a bit, then looked at his bike. He could see the front rim was twisted. Not good, he thought with a frown.

At the sound of a close, low growl, Seth whipped his head back around, which made the earth spin again.

Definitely not good.

Seth watched helplessly as a German shepherd the size of a pony came tearing at him.

Two

"Beau! Down!"

The animal stopped instantly at the woman's command and went into a crouch. Seth released the breath he'd been holding.

Good God, he thought. What next? A swarm of killer bees would rain down on him or maybe a meteor would fall out of the sky and he'd be right in its path?

"Good boy," Hannah said sweetly to the dog. "Stay."

Beau wagged his tail and obeyed Hannah's command, but his black eyes quickly darted back to the stranger.

"Nice dog you've got there." Seth kept a close eye on the animal.

"He belongs to Mrs. Peterson, but he's sort of adopted me and the girls. He'll be fine now." Hannah turned back around. "You don't have to worry."

"Did I say I was worried?" Seth said irritably. "I crash my motorcycle through fences, fall out of trees and face ferocious dogs all the time. Just another day in the life."

Hannah raised a brow. "You must have a very interesting life, Mr—"

"Granger. Seth Granger."

"Well, Mr. Granger," she said. "Since you're so determined to be up, why don't we get you inside? The doctor should be here shortly and he can take a look at that head of yours."

"There's nothing to look at," Seth insisted, then frowned when the woman smiled. "I mean, I'm *fine*."

"Maybe so, but it wouldn't hurt to—"

"Look." He brushed grass off his shirt. "I appreciate your concern, and I'm glad your little girl is all right. I'll just stop by a repair shop in town and have my bike checked, then be on my way."

Seth wasn't certain exactly what happened next. He'd taken a step toward his bike and his leg just went out from under him. Hannah gasped and made a lunge at him, but as her arms came around him, intended to stop his fall, she went down, too.

Because he couldn't stop it, he held her tight and brought her down on top of him, rather than underneath him.

Damn. This was the second time he'd found himself holding this woman close. She felt even better this time, with her body snug against his, lying on top of him. The heat of her skin seeped through his T-shirt and the feel of her long legs stretched out over his made the pain in his leg and the pounding in his head secondary.

At the sound of a low growl, Seth closed his eyes, then sighed heavily.

"All right," he said through clenched teeth. "You and Killer here win. I'll wait for the doc."

"You're a lucky man." Dr. Lansky, dressed in a blue plaid shirt and beige fisherman shorts, pushed his glasses up his nose as he stared at his patient's leg. "Looks like you've got just a nasty sprain instead of a break."

Since the doctor and Hannah had brought Seth into the house and settled him on the sofa, then stripped off his torn T-shirt and slit his jeans open to expose his ankle, he'd been surrounded by chaos. The phone had rung several times, neighbors had knocked on the door and a small crowd had gathered to watch Seth's motorcycle be towed away by the repair shop. His head was pounding like a drum and his leg hurt like a son of a bitch.

Of all the things that Seth felt, lucky was not one of them.

He ground his teeth together, struggling to hold back the swear words threatening to erupt. At least the cut on his head hadn't required stitches and the scratch on his shoulder was only superficial. He glanced at Hannah, who stood beside the sofa, her pretty lips pressed together with concern. Seth watched as two little blond, curly-topped heads—obviously twins—peeked from each side of their mother's hips and stared at him with big blue eyes.

With that blond hair and those blue eyes, Seth thought, there was no question the girls looked like their mother. Given all this commotion, Seth couldn't help but wonder where the twins' father was.

Seth glanced at Hannah's hand. No ring.

"We should X-ray to be sure, though." The balding

doctor continued to stare at Seth's swollen ankle.
"Can't be too careful, you know."

"I can drive him to the hospital," Hannah offered.
"Just let me get my—"

"That won't be necessary." Seth shook his head,
wished that he hadn't when a bolt of pain shot through
his skull. "It's not broken."

"So, Mr. Granger—" the doctor slipped his glasses
off and settled them in the pocket of his shirt "—along
with your ability to fly and scale tall trees in a single
bound, you also have X-ray vision?"

"I've had a broken bone or two." Four to be exact,
Seth thought, plus he'd been shot once and stabbed
twice. He'd be damned if he'd let a twisted ankle get
the better of him. "I'll be fine by the morning."

"I'm sure you will." The doctor took a prescription
pad out of the black leather bag he'd brought over. "In
the meantime, you might want to take some pain med-
ication. I recommend that you stay off that foot for several days."

"That's not possible. I need to get back on the road
right away."

Dr. Lansky ripped the prescription from his pad, then
handed it to Hannah. "I don't see any signs of concussion, but keep an eye on him, anyway. Clammy skin,
eyes dilated, confusion."

"Should I change the dressing over his eye?" she
asked.

"In the morning should be fine, you can—"

"Hey," Seth interrupted. "First of all, I'm sitting
right here, you can talk to me. Second, I can change my
own dressing. And third, I won't be here in the morning."

"Whatever you say." With raised eyebrows, the doctor glanced at Hannah, then looked at the two little girls and smiled. "Mrs. Lansky is outside passing out cookies. You girls want one?"

The children looked earnestly at their mother. Clearly they understood they'd caused all the commotion, but cookies were cookies, after all, and they could only hope.

Any other time, Hannah would have said absolutely not. Any other time, her daughters would be sitting in their room with a major time-out, probably until they were old enough to drive.

But the fact was, Hannah herself was still shaken by the afternoon's events. She needed a minute or two to gain her composure and every time she looked at Maddie, every time she thought about what might have happened, her hands started to shake.

She crossed her arms and gave Maddie and Missy her you-are-both-in-big-trouble look. "One cookie, then up to your rooms."

The girls skipped out ahead of the doctor, who cast one long, disapproving look at Seth, then went out the front door.

"I don't believe it." Seth laid his head back against the sofa and stared at the ceiling. "I crash my bike and your neighbors are out socializing in your front yard and passing around cookies. Probably fruitcake cookies."

"Probably chocolate chip, if Mrs. Lansky made them." Hannah moved closer to the couch. "Would you like one?"

He glanced up at her, and his narrowed, dark expression might have made her step away if she hadn't already figured out he wasn't nearly as dangerous as he appeared.

Well, at least, she didn't *think* he was.

She'd been so worried for the past hour, she hadn't taken the time to really look at the man. With his long legs and broad shoulders, he practically filled her small, rose floral sofa. Dr. Lansky had raised his patient's left leg onto her coffee table, and she'd slipped a sofa pillow under his sprained ankle. He hadn't complained once that he was in pain, but she'd seen a muscle twitch in his jaw when the doctor had asked him to bend his foot.

His hair was long, nearly to his shoulders, black and thick and shiny. His eyebrows, just as dark as his hair, slashed over eyes as hard and black as obsidian. His strong, square jaw hadn't been shaved for a while, which only added to that menacing look of his face, and underneath his firm, serious mouth, was a small, jagged scar.

She noticed another scar that sliced like a lightning bolt across his right bicep, let her gaze slide downward to his broad, bare chest, a chest lightly sprinkled with dark hair that narrowed downward over a hard, flat belly and disappeared behind the snap of his jeans.

Oh, my.

Hannah swallowed hard, then jerked her eyes back up to his face. Her heart skipped as he met her gaze with his own. His expression wasn't quite as fierce as it had been a moment ago, though it was certainly just as intense. She might have been offended at the blatant interest in his eyes if she hadn't been the one staring so hard at him.

"Mr. Granger—"

"Seth."

"Seth." She clasped her hands in front of her. "I don't know how to thank you for saving Maddie the way you did."

When he said nothing, just gave her a look that said he might have a suggestion or two, Hannah quickly continued. "I'm still not sure exactly what happened, but from what little I managed to gather, she'd accidentally tossed Suzie, her doll, up in the tree and it caught on a branch. Both of my daughters then conveniently forgot they aren't allowed to climb trees without adult supervision. If you hadn't come along when you did—"

"I did," Seth said with a shrug. "And she's fine."

"Yes." Hannah heard her daughters' laughter outside on the porch and said a silent prayer of thanks. "But you, however, and your motorcycle, are not. I'm deeply sorry for that, and any inconvenience we've caused you."

"Look," Seth sighed, "it's done, and it is what it is. I'll stay overnight in town, get my bike back in the morning and be on my way."

Hannah put a hand out to stop Seth when he lifted his leg and set it on the floor, but he ignored her warning. She watched as his jaw tightened, and his face went pale. The slow breath he exhaled pretty much said it all: he wasn't going anywhere on that leg. Not now, and not in the morning, either.

Men. They could be such fools at times.

"Seth." She sat on the sofa beside him and gently lifted his leg back up on the cushion. Perspiration beaded his forehead. "I admire your determination, but it might be time for you to consider a new plan. I have a suggestion."

"I can hardly wait to hear." Seth closed his eyes and laid his head back on the sofa.

"Good. Because you're going to."

One of his eyes slid open. Hannah ignored the frown

he gave her, then reached for the damp washcloth she'd laid on the coffee table and dabbed at his forehead.

He reached up and wrapped his hand around her upper arm.

Breath held, she waited for him to release her, but he didn't. Both of his eyes were open now, that dark, intense gaze completely focused on her.

Hannah felt her pulse race as he continued to stare silently at her. His hand moved slowly up her arm; the texture of his callused palm on her skin sent ripples of electricity shimmering through her body.

She stared back at him, too startled to move, too startled even to speak. She'd never experienced anything like this before. Never experienced anything like *him*. When his gaze drifted to her mouth, her insides fluttered. The heat of his body, the masculine scent of his skin, overwhelmed her.

Time stopped. Time and a sense of where she was, who she was, and certainly who she was with. Nothing seemed to exist but this moment, this incredible heart-stopping, mind-blowing instant. If she'd had the presence of mind, she would have pulled away, would have even been offended at the brazen stroke of his thumb on her arm. But she didn't pull away. She wasn't offended.

She was turned on.

Her skin felt hot, she had trouble breathing and her breasts ached.

How is this possible? Hannah asked herself numbly. She certainly wasn't the kind of woman who could be turned on by a stranger—she wasn't even the kind of woman who was turned on by men she *knew,* for heaven's sake. She'd accepted the fact long ago that she wasn't like most women. Sex, when she'd been married, had been all right, she supposed, but she'd never understood what all the hoopla had been about.

"So what do you suggest I do?"

"What?" Hannah blinked, stared at Seth, then blinked again. She had all kinds of suggestions, none of which she would have had the courage to speak out loud. "Suggest?"

"You said you have a suggestion." His hand slid up to her wrist, then he tugged the washcloth from her fingers and tossed it on the coffee table. "So what is it?"

A suggestion? Hannah struggled to gain her composure and remember exactly what she'd said before he'd touched her and turned her world upside down.

"I—you...well—" Hannah felt her cheeks flush, knew she sounded like a babbling idiot. So she just blurted it out. "You can stay here."

"Here?" He tilted a look at her. "You mean in your house?"

"Yes." Her pulse was still racing, but her breathing was nearly back to normal, thank goodness. "I've been converting my house to a bed-and-breakfast for the past six months. I only have two more bedrooms to finish and then I can open for business. You can stay in one of the rooms I've finished."

He stared at her for what felt like minutes, though it was only seconds. She waited, breath held, until he finally said, "You'd let a complete stranger stay in your house?"

"I realize how naive that sounds," Hannah said evenly. "But after what you did, the way you never even gave a thought to yourself when you saved Maddie, the way you talked to her when you climbed out on that branch, well, I'm certain you're a person I can trust. I'll just consider you the first guest of the Wild Rose.''

''The Wild Rose?''

''That's what I'm going to call my bed-and-breakfast,'' Hannah said. ''You won't even have to walk up any stairs. I have two finished guest rooms on the ground floor. You can have your pick.''

''Hannah.'' Seth shook his head. ''You don't know anything about me.''

''Well, actually, that's not completely true.'' Hannah shifted awkwardly. ''Mrs. Peterson found your wallet on my front lawn. She insisted that it was lying open and she 'just happened' to notice your Albuquerque police badge.''

He lifted a brow. '''Just happened' to notice?''

Hannah reached for the wallet sitting on the end table. ''Along with the fact that you're single, thirty years old, six-foot-four, with black eyes and black hair.''

''I'm surprised she didn't 'just happen' to notice my weight and the fact that I'm an organ donor, too,'' he said sarcastically.

''Actually, she did. I'm sorry.'' Her cheeks turned pink as she handed him the wallet. ''You're already a bit of a celebrity here. Billy Bishop from the *Ridgewater Gazette* wants to do a cover story on you.''

Terrific. Seth held back on the groan threatening to surface. Jarris would just love hearing that one of his undercover detectives had his picture plastered on the front page of this backwater town. Throw in the story about how he'd broken his superior's nose after a bad bust last week, then how he'd been suspended for six weeks, and Jarris would probably be so happy he'd burst a blood vessel.

''No story. You tell Billy Bob—''

"Billy Bishop."

"Whatever. You tell him absolutely, positively, *no story.*"

"I'll try," Hannah said hesitantly. "But you don't know Billy."

"Let's keep it that way." Seth stared at the bag of frozen peas covering his ankle. As much as he hated to admit it, his foot hurt like hell. He didn't like it, but he knew he had to face the fact that he wasn't going anywhere today and probably not tomorrow, either. "I'll need to speak to the tow-truck driver before he leaves. I'll need some kind of time frame on the repairs."

"I'll go see if he's still here." Hannah stood, glanced toward the front door and the sound of people talking outside. "I—I am sorry about all this. My daughters are usually very well behaved, but sometimes they act up when—" she hesitated, then drew in a slow breath "—when there's a lot going on."

Seth could tell that Hannah had been about to say one thing, then quickly changed her mind. He admitted it made him curious, but he shrugged it off. Whatever she'd been about to say was none of his business. Unless a person was a criminal or under investigation, he made it a rule never to interfere or pry into anyone's life. He figured if he didn't want people butting into his life, then he should keep his nose out of their business, as well.

But there was one thing he wanted to know, though. One thing he felt he *needed* to know. He glanced at her ringless hand again, but wasn't about to make any assumptions.

"Will your husband have a problem with me staying here?"

She stilled at his question, then slowly shook her head. "I'm divorced. It's just me and the girls here."

Since he wouldn't be around more than a couple of days, Seth knew it shouldn't matter to him one way or the other, but the fact she was divorced pleased him. He supposed he just didn't like the idea of lusting after a married woman. Though he didn't have many rules in his life, there were a few he never broke.

"So you're opening a bed-and-breakfast all by your-self?"

"Not exactly. My friend, Lori, is going to work with me two or three days a week, plus Mrs. Peterson next door has already offered her help if I need it. I'm not foolish enough to think I'll have full occupancy the minute I open my doors, but there's only one motel in town and we get quite a few people traveling through here."

"Looking for the world's largest fruitcake?"

She smiled, didn't seem to take offense at the slight mocking tone in his voice. "As simple as it might sound to you, the giant fruitcake Wilhem's Bakery bakes once a year is this town's claim to fame. Most of the people who live here take it very seriously. And believe it or not, we get our fair share of tourists. With only one small motel in Ridgewater, I should be able to make a living, at least enough to support me and the girls."

She turned at the knock on her front door. Her ex-pression was apologetic when she looked back at him.

"My neighbors kept a respectable distance while the doctor was in here with you," she said with a sigh. "But they can only be held at bay for so long. Whether you like it or not, you're a hero, Mr. Granger, and the town of Ridgewater, Texas, home of the world's largest fruitcake, is about to welcome you."

Three

Hannah kept a safe distance from Seth for the rest of the evening. Not that she could have gotten close to him even if she'd wanted to. The town's phone wires had been burning up since Detective Granger had plowed through her fence and rescued Maddie, and there'd been a steady stream of people coming through the house for the past two hours to meet this mystery man. And though Hannah certainly didn't approve, Maddie and Missy were the belles of the ball, receiving as much attention as Seth, with everyone telling them what brave little girls they were and patting them on the head. The twins were eating it up and had been eager to retell the incident over and over, embellishing the story each time, until it appeared that Seth truly was the man of steel.

The only thing missing was his red cape and a big *S* on his chest.

While Maddie and Missy sat together on a chair in the living room and told their story one more time to Helen Myers, a waitress at the town's diner, Hannah stood by the kitchen door and watched Billy Bishop attempt to pump Seth for information. Though he'd been stiffly polite to the people who had come to meet and gawk at a real, live superhero, Seth was having no part of Billy's questions.

He still sat on the sofa, his leg on display as if it were a war monument, his face looking as if it might crack at any moment. Everyone oohed and ahhed and shook their heads with sympathy while Billy asked Seth what he'd been thinking when he'd so selflessly snatched Maddie from the tree branch. Seth glared at the twenty-three-year-old, spiky-blond-haired reporter, and Hannah doubted that Billy really wanted to know what Seth was obviously thinking at the moment.

Like it or not—and clearly he didn't—Seth Granger was big news in Ridgewater. Outside of barbed wire and armed guards, Hannah could see no way to keep her neighbors and townspeople away.

At least they'd come prepared, she thought as she looked at her dining-room table. At present count, she'd received three casseroles, a broccoli-bacon salad, two apple pies, a pecan coffee cake and one half-frozen fruitcake. Since Hannah had set out plates, silverware and coffee, the noise level in the room had dropped several decibels while people ate.

"I saw the whole thing," Hannah heard Mrs. Peterson tell George Fitzer, who'd just arrived on the scene and was filling a plate with macaroni and cheese. "He was amazing. Truly amazing."

"We should give him a trophy," Mrs. Hinkle, the town librarian said.

"For heaven's sake, Mildred." Mrs. Peterson rolled her eyes. "The man didn't bowl a perfect game, he saved a child."

"Well, maybe a medal, then." Mrs. Hinkle reached for the last piece of coffee cake. "Or a plaque."

"I know what *I'd* like to give him."

Startled, Hannah turned at the sound of the voice behind her, saw the look of appraisal in her best friend's eyes as she stared at Seth.

"Lori Simpson," Hannah whispered over her shoulder, "shame on you. You're a married woman and mother of three."

"What?" Lori, a pretty redhead with big green eyes, gave Hannah an expression of complete innocence. "I was going to say a coconut cream pie."

Hannah lifted one brow in doubt.

Lori stared across the room and grinned. "And after I smeared the whipped cream all over his body, I'd slowly lick it all off and—"

"Stop." Hannah felt her cheeks start to warm. In fact, she felt her entire body start to warm at the image Lori had just given her. "You have a gorgeous husband who adores you. How can you talk like that?"

"Oh, Hannah, I'm kidding." Lori looked back at Seth. "Sort of. And for heaven's sake, it's not as if I'd ever do anything like that. Well, except with John, of course. That man is absolutely amazing in the bedroom. Just last week he—"

"*Stop!*" Hannah put a hand over Lori's mouth. The last thing Hannah wanted to hear about right now was her best friend's bedroom escapades. She didn't want to hear about *anyone's* bedroom activities, for that matter. Since her own sex life was so abysmal, it was better to simply leave that subject alone. "Where's John?"

"He's home with the kids. Patrick is working on his one-year molars and Nickie, my little drama queen, had a wart burned off her pinkie today and is walking around as if the doctor had amputated." Lori watched Elma Thumple walk in with a plate of brownies and snagged one as the woman passed by. "Bless his heart, John offered to stay home so I could come over and meet the man who saved my goddaughter's life. So give me details. Tell Auntie Lori exactly what happened."

Lori might not officially be Maddie and Missy's aunt, Hannah thought, but Lori had been through the worst of everything with Hannah for the three years since her divorce. Hannah didn't know how she would have made it through everything without Lori's friendship. As far as Hannah was concerned, Lori was as real a sister to her as if they had shared a mother.

"Maybe later, Lor." Hannah shook her head, blinked at the sudden moisture in her eyes. "It's been a long day. A tough one."

"Oh, honey." Lori frowned and slipped an arm around Hannah's shoulders. "Knowing this town, I assumed the accounts had been grossly exaggerated when you hadn't called me yourself."

"I—I was just so…dazed. And frightened. It all happened so fast." Darn it, where were these tears coming from? The last thing she needed was to start blubbering in front of all these people. "I'm sorry."

"Never mind." Lori hugged her. "We'll talk later, over a bottle of wine and a box of tissues."

Hannah had replayed the scene over and over in her mind at least a hundred times in the past three hours: Seth climbing out on that branch while Maddie hung in midair, Seth pulling Maddie up, then handing her over. The crack of the branch and Seth falling. Every single time those images flipped through her brain, Hannah felt her breath catch and her heart stop.

She looked at Seth now, and once again her heart stopped. Only this time, it was because he was looking at her.

And there it was again.

She felt frozen. Absolutely consumed and completely overwhelmed. Helpless to do anything but stare back at him.

She felt the deep, heavy thud of her heart, heard the din of conversation around her, but she simply couldn't move. Nothing like this had ever happened to her before. She felt stripped naked, and yet, she just didn't care.

She knew she'd been unsteady all afternoon. After what had happened, it was understandable that her emotions would be spiralling.

But this was more than that.

This was something much more.

The thought frightened her. She didn't want to be attracted to this man. At this point in her life, she didn't want to be attracted to *any* man.

He held her gaze with his and still she didn't look away.

He was handsome, of course, though a little rough around the edges. But that only seemed to add to his appeal. The stubble of beard on that strong jaw and square chin, that thick mane of black hair touching those broad shoulders, the faded jeans over his long, muscled legs. He'd changed into a clean T-shirt, also black, and Hannah realized how well the color suited him. Everything about this man was dark and dangerous, and with that bandage over his eye, he bordered on ominous.

He radiated sex. Made her think things she didn't want to think about, things she'd thought hadn't mattered to her: a man's touch, urgent whispers in the dark, sweaty bodies and twisted sheets.

As if he read her thoughts, Seth's eyes narrowed and grew more intense as he stared at her.

Dear Lord, had she actually asked this man to *stay* with her? Hannah thought. Here, in this house, where during the day, while the girls were at school, she would be *alone* with him?

Hannah rarely drank anything alcoholic, but suddenly she was wishing for a glass of that wine Lori had mentioned a moment ago.

"Hannah, sweetheart," Lori whispered in Hannah's ear, "you keep staring at Mr. Handsome like that and this room is going to self-combust."

Hannah quickly looked away. "I have no idea what you're talking about."

"Right." Lori smiled and took a bite of brownie. "I guess I just imagined that I'd-like-to-rip-your-clothes-off-and-jump-on-you look in your eyes."

"Lori Simpson." Hannah snatched the brownie from her friend's hand and bit into the rich chocolate. "Do you ever think of anything besides sex?"

Lori thought for a moment.

"Oh, for heaven's sake." Hannah shook her head. "It was a foolish question. Never mind."

Maddie and Missy spotted Lori at that moment and came running over. While they related their terrible ordeal once again, Hannah slipped into the kitchen.

Thankful for the quiet, Hannah set about making a fresh pot of coffee. She just needed a few moments alone, away from all the commotion in her house.

Away from Seth.

I can do this, Hannah told herself as she counted out scoops of coffee into the pot. Everything would be back to normal by the morning. She'd bake muffins for the diner and drop them off on her way to carpool the girls to school, pick up the accounting work she did weekly for Tom Wheeler and do her data entry, then repair the cracks on the walls in the upstairs bedroom. By the time Maddie and Missy came home from school, it would be time for homework, supper, baths and bedtime stories for the girls, then the rest of the evening she could work on the hand-stitching Lyn Gross had hired her to do for her catalog business.

As if she had time to think about handsome strangers and her out-of-whack hormones. Hannah laughed at her own foolishness as she filled the glass carafe with water. Besides, she had a very large house. She'd be working upstairs, Seth would be downstairs. She probably wouldn't even see him, except in passing. It wasn't as if he could get around very well, anyway.

She didn't have the time or the desire to be distracted by Seth Granger. He'd be gone in a few days and her house would be back to normal—not that *normal* would in any way describe her life, she thought, shaking her head with a smile.

Once she had her bed-and-breakfast open for business, Hannah would have everything she wanted: her own business, security for Maddie and Missy, and once she bought out Aunt Martha's share of the house, a sense of independence she'd never had before.

There wasn't anything else she wanted at this point in her life. She'd done just fine without a man for the past three years. In the future, maybe she would meet someone. A man who wanted roots and family and came home at night. Before midnight, without another woman's perfume on his shirt.

For now, Hannah only needed Maddie and Missy and that was enough. Seth Granger might be an interesting and temporary diversion, Hannah admitted, but that's all he was: interesting and temporary, with the emphasis on temporary.

While the coffee percolated, Hannah opened the refrigerator to refill the creamer she'd set out on the table. Beside the container of half and half was a can of whipped cream someone had brought to go with a bowl of strawberries.

...*I'd like to smear it all over his body and lick it off*...

Hannah slammed the refrigerator door shut and forced the image Lori had given her out of her mind. Her heart pounded against her ribs.

Suddenly her house didn't seem large enough at all, and a few days felt like a very, very long time.

The scent of hot cinnamon roused Seth during the night. Darkness surrounded him and he wasn't certain where he was, but that wasn't so unusual. He'd woken up more than once in the dark in a strange place, a strange bed. In his line of work, he was never certain about where he'd be sleeping. A car, a park bench, even an occasional alley, amidst a community of homeless who lived in cardboard structures and tents made out of blankets. Wherever his job took him, he went, and most of the time it seemed as if he spent more time on the streets than in his own apartment.

But the scent of cinnamon and...what else? Apples, that's what it was. The scent of cinnamon and apples had never woken him before. For several moments, he thought he might be dreaming, maybe having one of the flashbacks he occasionally had from his childhood. Before the accident. Before his life had changed so dramatically.

But he wasn't dreaming, he realized. The scent was very real, as real as the bed he lay in. A firm, comfortable mattress covered with smooth, soft sheets, feather pillows and a thick, down comforter. He blinked, raised his head and glanced at the bedside clock.

Five in the morning. Not exactly the middle of the night, but not exactly what he'd call morning, either.

Seth blinked again, rolled to his back and felt the pain shoot straight up his leg.

He swore hotly and remembered where he was.

In Ridgewater, Texas.

Home of the world's largest fruitcake.

Gritting his teeth, Seth slid his legs out from under the covers and sat on the edge of the bed. When the pain subsided, he flipped on the nightstand lamp and looked around the room. It was a nice room, large, with high ceilings and white chair rails against soft blue-and-white striped walls. The windows were tall with lace curtains, the highly polished hardwood floors dotted with navy blue throw rugs. There was a white-tiled bathroom attached to the room, with a ball-and-claw bathtub and a showerhead that a guest could hold or attach to the wall.

Seth dragged a hand through his hair and stretched, then rolled his shoulders. His neck felt a little stiff and a low throb pounded in his head, but all in all, other than his swollen ankle, which had turned a deep shade of purple, he felt fine.

Well, as fine as he could feel about being stuck in the middle of nowhere for God knew how long.

After last night's gathering, Seth was counting the minutes until he could leave Ridgewater. He knew he should appreciate that all those people had shown up to meet him, but the fact was, he didn't. He hadn't done anything that any other person in his situation wouldn't have done. He didn't deserve, and he sure as hell didn't like, all that attention.

Especially from Billy Bishop, ace reporter for the *Ridgewater Gazette.*

Billy had been a major pain in the butt. He'd wanted to know every detail of Seth's life. His work, his past, even his hobbies, for God's sake. Even if he had a hobby, which he didn't, who the hell would care what it was? He'd intentionally kept his answers vague and short. The less he gave Billy Bob Bishop, the shorter the article and the quicker this entire incident would fade away.

Careful not to put any pressure on his ankle, he slipped out of bed and pulled on a pair of gray sweat pants and the T-shirt he'd worn the night before, then hobbled to the door and followed the seductive scent to the kitchen. He paused in the doorway, surprised to see Hannah standing at the counter, filling muffin tins with thick batter from a large metal bowl. From a big blue clip on top of her head, her long blond curls tumbled down her back like a rippling waterfall. She wore a light-blue robe and pink bunny slippers. He could swear she was humming...

..."Born to be Wild?"

Smiling, he leaned against the doorjamb and watched her. After she'd shown him to his room last night, she'd laid out fresh towels and soap, apologized for all the commotion, then quickly excused herself. She'd inten-

tionally avoided eye contact with him, even as she was
thanking him once again for saving Maddie.

He supposed she'd been nervous about him staying
in the house. He was a complete stranger to her, after
all, and the only thing she really knew about him, other
than his driver's license statistics, was that he worked
for the Albuquerque police department.

But earlier in the evening, when she'd been talking
to her friend, Seth had looked at her. And she'd looked
back.

Whatever had passed between them—and he still
wasn't certain if he'd imagined it—had been potent.

It wasn't as if he hadn't experienced lust before. Hell,
that was more than familiar territory to him. What
hadn't been familiar had been the intensity of what
should have been a simple look, but had been anything
but simple. And while it disturbed him on one level, it
intrigued him on another.

She intrigued him. A beautiful woman, single mother
of mischievous twin girls, soon-to-be proprietor of a
bed-and-breakfast. He'd seen the fear in her pale-blue
eyes yesterday when he'd handed Maddie to her, but
she'd stayed calm and kept her composure when a lot
of women would have come unraveled. She'd taken
care of him, then graciously opened her house to her
neighbors, quietly set out coffee and food and stood
back and watched.

Her song changed from Steppenwolf to Ricky Mar-
tin's "Shake Your Bon-Bon." Seth dropped his gaze to
her pretty bottom moving back and forth to the Latin
beat, and he felt his gut tighten. Damn. He'd never been
a fan of Ricky's until this moment.

Seth swallowed the dryness in his throat, knew that
he should announce his presence rather than standing

here leering at the woman. He just couldn't help himself. The sight of her moving to the song, dressed in that simple bathrobe and bunny slippers should have been humorous, but strangely, he found it sexy. When she gave an extra little twist to her hips, Seth forgot to breathe.

Damn if the woman wasn't getting him hard.

He supposed the fall might have rattled his brain, but whatever it was, his hormones had jumped to attention and were clanging warning bells. His pulse quickened, and it seemed as if all the blood from his head had taken a trip south.

He remembered the firm press of her body against his yesterday, the smooth feel of her skin under his hands when he'd held her arm on the sofa, the way she'd looked at him last night across the crowded room. No question there was chemistry between them.

The question was, should he act on it?

Strange, but he'd never asked himself that before. If he'd wanted a woman and she'd wanted him, it was simple. If it felt right, Seth had never held back. He went for it and whatever happened, happened.

But Hannah wasn't simple. Something told him that she was anything *but* simple. Seth knew he was just passing through this town and this woman's life. The last thing he should be doing was having thoughts about taking her to bed.

Then she shook her bottom again as she softly sang and Seth felt as if he'd been punched in the gut. He knew if he didn't stop her, he was probably going to do something very foolish.

"Morning."

She whirled around, a look of sheer shock on her

face. She stood there for a moment, eyes wide as she stared at him, then her face flushed bright red.

Because she hadn't belted her robe, the short, pink cotton nightgown she had on didn't hide much. At the sight of her high, unfettered breasts, he felt another slam to his gut. His gaze traveled down over her long, shapely legs, and his body flooded with heat.

Even her silly slippers looked sexy to him, an obvious indication he wasn't thinking clearly. He could picture himself tugging those bunnies off her feet, then sliding his hand up her sleek curves, over her hips and under her simple cotton nightgown, up higher, until his palms were filled with her soft, feminine flesh.

It took a few seconds and a will of iron to wrench his gaze back up to hers. She still hadn't moved, except that her lips had formed a small O.

When he pushed away from the doorjamb, she instantly went from zero to eighty. She mumbled a good morning as she whipped back around, dropped the batter-filled measuring cup into the bowl, then belted her bathrobe tightly.

"I wasn't expecting you up this early," she said over her shoulder, her voice strained and high-pitched. "I hope I didn't wake you."

Oh, she'd wakened him all right. His entire body was awake and alert and ready to go. "Actually, it was those muffins you're baking."

He hobbled to the large oak table in the middle of the spacious kitchen. Hannah quickly reached for a towel to wipe her hands.

"You shouldn't be up on that leg," she said firmly and rushed to his side to slip an arm around his waist.

"I'm fine, Hannah."

But he let her help him into the chair, not because

he needed help, but because he wanted to indulge himself, if only for a moment. He felt the soft press of her breasts against his side and nearly groaned at the rush of heat through his body. He breathed in the scent of apples and cinnamon on her skin, held on to her longer than was necessary or wise. When she moved away, it was all he could do not to snatch her back and see if she tasted as good as she smelled.

She pulled a second chair beside him and gently raised his leg onto the checkered cushioned seat pad. She knelt at his feet, plumping the cushion, and hadn't realized her robe had opened at the top, revealing the twin points of her nipples through the thin cotton.

"How does that feel?" she asked.

He desperately wanted to know exactly what they would feel like in his hands, in his mouth, but he tore his gaze from her breasts and swallowed hard. "Fine," he said through clenched teeth. "I'm just fine. Go back to what you were doing."

Quickly, he thought. *Before I show you just how fine I really am.*

The timer on the stove started to buzz and to his relief, she hurried to the oven and pulled out a pan of baked muffins. That's when he glanced around the kitchen and realized there were several dozen muffins already out on the counter.

"Are you expecting another mob this morning?" he asked incredulously.

She smiled as she set the pan on the counter. "I bake these every weekday morning for the diner in town and deliver them when I take the girls to school. Would you like blueberry, banana, or apple spice?"

Good Lord, what time did she get up in the morning?

Seth wondered. There had to be at least eight dozen muffins on her counter. "Apple spice."

The muffin she set in front of him was still hot. When he broke it open, a fragrant cloud of steam drifted upward. Seth breathed in the spicy scent, then bit in.

He closed his eyes on a groan. When he opened them again, she was watching him, a smile on her pretty lips.

"It's all right?" she asked.

"All right?" He took another bite. "Damn, woman, but this has got to be the best muffin I ever ate."

Her smile widened. "Thank you."

The expression of pure pleasure on her face only fueled Seth's hunger, a hunger that had nothing to do with muffins or with food at all, for that matter. It had everything to do with lust and the arousal that had him shifting in his seat before he embarrassed her even more.

"I—I'll put some coffee on," she said after a long moment and turned away, but not before he saw the same thing in her eyes that he was feeling.

Desire.

He hadn't imagined it, and it certainly wasn't one-sided. She wanted him just as much as he wanted her.

He stared at her back, noticed the stiffness in her shoulders, the slight shaking of her hands as she measured out the coffee.

So what the hell was he going to do about it? They were two adults, moving in different directions with different lives. but they both knew that. If they ended up in bed together, even briefly, what was the harm in that?

Probably none, he thought, but the dark, heavy tension between them made him edgy, made him uncertain. There were some things he didn't like being uncertain about. Meeting a snitch in a dark alley, walking into a room undercover without backup, sitting with his back to a window. He didn't like shadows, places where people could hide or blend in.

Hannah felt like a shadow to him. A sexy, enticing one, but a shadow all the same. She made him nervous, kept him off balance. He needed control at all times, in his life, in his job, and definitely in his relationships.

With a sigh, he turned his attention back to the muffin. He reminded himself he needed to get to Wolf River, that he had a family waiting for him. That's what he needed to concentrate on right now. What he *wanted* to concentrate on.

He might be held up a couple of days, but as soon as he got his motorcycle back, he'd hit the road again, and pretty little Hannah Michaels would be nothing more than a pleasant memory.

Four

"Three dozen blueberry, three dozen banana, four dozen apple spice." Phoebe Harmon signed the check she'd filled out and slid it across her desk to Hannah. "Can you manage a special order for an extra six dozen tomorrow? The Chamber of Commerce is hosting career day at the high school."

"No problem." It would mean getting up an hour early, but Hannah was happy for the extra few dollars it would bring her. "Is assorted all right?"

"Assorted is fine."

Phoebe, a full-figured platinum blonde in her fifties, had married Duke Harmon ten years ago and together they'd opened Duke's Diner. Phoebe was one hell of a cook, but she didn't bake. All of the desserts served at Duke's were brought in from the locals. Shirley Gordon made the pies and cookies, Hannah made the muffins and special-order cakes.

"So I heard you had quite a scare yesterday." True concern shone in Phoebe's big, brown eyes. "How're the girls doing today?"

"They're fine." Hannah dropped the check in her purse and glanced at her watch. "And they're going to be late for school if I don't get going."

"Oh, come on, Hannah." Phoebe pouted. "You've got a minute. Just give me the juicy details. Is he really staying with you?"

Hannah sighed. She'd known, of course, that sooner or later the entire town would find out that Seth was staying with her, but she'd hoped it would take longer than twelve hours for word to spread.

"Just for a few days," she said politely. "Until his ankle is better and his motorcycle is repaired."

"So tell me, honey—" Phoebe leaned across the desk and raised one brow "—is he married?"

"No."

"Engaged?"

"Not that I know of."

Phoebe's face lit up. "Under fifty?"

"Yes." Hannah leaned in and whispered, "And you know what else?"

Breath held, Phoebe stretched her neck closer. "What?"

"I even think he's got all his own teeth."

Phoebe pressed her bright red lips into a thin line and sat back. "Don't be sassy, Hannah Michaels. You're a businesswoman. As a businesswoman, you should make the most of any and all opportunities presented to you. Don't you want a man to warm your bed and be a daddy to your girls?"

"I have an electric blanket, Phoebe, and the girls are doing just fine."

"Pshaw. You're a young woman. It's about time you snagged yourself a husband." Phoebe grinned and wiggled her heavily lined eyebrows. "Or at least time that you did the mattress mambo."

Hannah felt her cheeks warm at Phoebe's comment. As if it wasn't bad enough that her best friend was harping at her, now Phoebe was jumping on the bandwagon, too. Next thing she knew they'd form a committee and have weekly meetings to discuss poor Hannah Michaels's sex life.

Or should she say, her *lack* of a sex life.

"Just do an old broad a favor and tell me what he's like, honey," Phoebe said with a wink. "From what I heard, the man is sexy as sin."

Sex and sin, Hannah thought. Two appropriate words to describe Seth Granger. In her mind, she could still see him standing in her kitchen doorway this morning, wearing sweat pants and a T-shirt, his handsome face unshaven and his long hair rumpled. Just the image made her pulse quicken and her breath catch.

Had he been watching her? she'd wondered. She always enjoyed listening to music when she baked or worked around the house and sometimes she got a little carried away. The thought that he might have seen her acting so silly made the blush already on her cheeks burn hotter.

How could she have guessed he would be up so early? And how absolutely ridiculous she must have looked to him, dancing around in her old robe and nightgown and bunny slippers. Hannah Michaels: femme fatale.

Well, it didn't matter what he thought of her, she decided. Why should it? It wasn't as if anything was going to happen between them. Just because she'd noticed the man's biceps and chest, and just because she'd fantasized about him—just a little—after she'd gone to bed last night, well, that didn't mean she was going to *sleep* with him, for heaven's sake.

She owed him a place to stay, that was all. So maybe there was a little chemistry between them—so okay, maybe a *lot* of chemistry—but she had Maddie and Missy to think about, along with a hundred other things, like baking muffins and sanding the upstairs bedroom and finishing the accounting work on her desk. She needed to stay focused, in control. Thinking about Seth Granger left her out of balance and confused.

"Hello, I'm waiting here," Phoebe said and broke into Hannah's wandering thoughts. "Come on, Hannah. You're a beautiful gal, he's a handsome stud, both of you sleeping under the same roof. That must at least get the juices flowing."

"I've been able to control my carnal appetites," Hannah said.

"Well, that's no fun." Phoebe frowned. "Come on, Hannah, give me something. Tell me he's at least made a pass at you."

"No, he has not."

The utter disappointment on Phoebe's face nearly made Hannah laugh. She supposed she could leave the woman with a *little* something.

Hannah glanced over her shoulder, then lowered her voice and leaned close to Phoebe. "But I will tell you one thing, as long as you promise not to tell anyone else."

Phoebe brightened, ran her pinched fingers over her mouth as if she were closing a zipper.

Hannah leaned closer and whispered, "He likes my apple spice muffins."

Phoebe straightened and folded her arms over her chest. "Hannah Michaels, you aren't too old to turn over my knee, you know. I went to high school with your mama."

Laughing, Hannah turned and waggled her fingers as she walked out of the diner. In spite of Phoebe's disappointment, Hannah was certain that the woman would make the best of what little Hannah had given her to talk about.

There was no doubt in Hannah's mind that by tomorrow, the orders for her apple spice muffins would be double.

Seth tried to watch TV in his room after Hannah took her daughters to school at eight o'clock, but other than a sports game or a movie with lots of explosions and car crashes, he'd never been much interested in television. With the long hours he normally worked, he was rarely home long enough to do anything more than sleep and eat.

He'd heard Hannah return shortly after nine, but thought it best to stay in his room out of her way. He'd channel-surfed for the past three hours, watched bits and pieces of at least twenty different shows and an entire episode of "I Love Lucy."

Saturated with daytime programming, he shut the TV off and used his cell phone to call the auto body shop that had towed his bike away yesterday. A recorded message stated they would not be open until noon, and would answer all calls as soon as possible.

Noon? Seth scowled at the phone for several seconds. What kind of business didn't open until noon, for crying out loud!

Annoyed, he bit his tongue, then left a message and

his cell-phone number. He understood that small towns ran at a slower pace, but this was ridiculous.

He stared at the blue stripes on the wall for a few minutes, but when those walls started to close in on him, he decided he'd had enough. Gritting his teeth, he stripped off his sweats, carefully slipped on a pair of clean jeans, then dropped his cell phone into his T-shirt pocket and hobbled into the living room.

The fresh scent of lemon wax and disinfectant greeted him. He realized Hannah had been cleaning downstairs while he'd been in his room all morning. He heard the sound of music from an upstairs bedroom and considered dragging himself up the stairs to see what she was up to, then decided against it. Instead, he found a novel by John Grisham on one of her bookshelves that he'd been meaning to read for a long time and settled himself down on the sofa. After a few minutes he realized that he'd read page six four times and slapped the book shut.

Sitting around doing nothing was bad enough, but sitting around doing nothing while Hannah fluttered busily around the house was making him…nutty as a fruitcake.

He frowned at the expression that had popped into his brain. Dammit, he *had* hit his head too hard.

Listening to the music made him wonder what she was doing. He heard the unmistakable sound of masking tape being ripped off a roll, then the rasp of sandpaper. He stared at the stairs, then pressed his lips together firmly. He wasn't going up there, dammit. If he caught sight of her shaking that cute bottom of hers again, he might lose it completely.

Some fresh air would take his mind off Hannah Michaels, Seth decided. Yeah, right. Some fresh air, along with a bottle of whiskey.

The day was warming quickly, but the covered front porch was cool. Hannah had placed several large clay pots of green plants beside two white wicker chairs and two small ferns inside a wooden, decorative wheelbarrow. The front leaded windows were tall and sparkling clean, the front door and trim all painted white to contrast with the blue house. A pretty picture, he thought, just like the house's owner.

What wasn't so pretty was the broken tree branch still lying in the middle of Hannah's front yard, or the smashed slats of wooden fencing he'd crashed through yesterday. There'd been no way to avoid the damage, but still he felt bad that she'd have to deal with the repairs. The least he could do was clean the mess up, he thought.

Grabbing hold of the porch rail, Seth hopped down the steps on one leg and made his way to the branch. He paid no attention to the numerous cars that slowed to a crawl as they drove by. He dragged the broken limb to the side of Hannah's yard, then inside the fence that was still standing, he piled the broken slats of wood, determined to ignore the throb in his ankle. In spite of the pain, it felt good to do something.

"What exactly do you think you're doing?"

Startled, Seth turned at the sound of Hannah's voice behind him. She stood on the sidewalk, hands on her denim-clad hips, a frown furrowing her brow.

Damn if she didn't look pretty, he thought, standing there staring sternly at him with those baby-blue eyes. She'd pulled her hair back into some kind of braid, but several long golden strands had escaped and curled around her flushed face. The white sleeveless blouse she wore revealed long slender arms, arms she now tucked under her breasts in a gesture of disapproval. As much as he wanted to admire her womanly attributes, he forced his attention to stay on her face.

"I distinctly heard the doctor tell you that you need to rest and stay off that foot." She glanced around the yard and shook her head. "Dragging tree branches around and piling wood does not fit into either category."

"I needed some fresh air." He tossed a piece of cracked wood into the pile he'd made, then straightened. "And I've been resting all morning. If my ankle starts to bother me, I assure you I'll stay off it."

"You should have called me." She pressed her lips firmly together. "I would have opened a window, or at least helped you outside."

"I'm fine, Hannah." He bent over and picked up a chunk of wood. "I'm absolutely fine."

To prove it, he put his full weight on his foot and stepped toward the pile of wood.

And crumpled like a dry leaf.

For the second time in two days, Seth found himself flat on his back staring up at blue sky. This time, though, there were stars in that blue sky, and he waited a moment for the pain to subside. As if his embarrassment and frustration weren't enough, a car driving by at that moment stopped.

"Need some help there?" a man called out.

Hannah smiled and waved. "No thanks, Mr. Langdon. Mr. Granger here is just resting his ankle."

Seth counted to ten while the man and Hannah talked about Maddie and the accident and then the man told Seth to keep up the good work and drove off.

Hannah stood over him and stared down, but made

no move to help him up. Amusement sparkled in her eyes, and he thought about dragging her down on top of him.

Instead, he glared up at her.

"Are you always this difficult?" she asked.

"Absolutely not." He sat slowly and brushed grass from his sleeves. "Usually I'm much worse. You've caught me on a good day."

"Lucky me." Shaking her head, she knelt beside him. "Now are you going to behave, or shall I call in the heavy artillery?"

He lifted a brow. "And that is?"

"For starters, I'll call the doctor and tattle on you, then I'll invite Billy Bishop over and tell him you're giving him an exclusive, then I'll tell Mrs. Schwartz that you're bored and would love it if her bingo group came over, then—"

"All right, all right." He held up a hand and sighed. "You win. I'll behave. Are you always this hard-hearted?"

"Absolutely not." She smiled and offered her hand. "You caught me on a good day."

In spite of everything, Seth grinned at her. He took her hand and let her help him up. Her fingers were soft against his palm, yet her grip was amazingly strong. He had a sharp, clear image of those hands on his body and felt himself harden at the thought.

Another car drove by and honked, smashing his image to smithereens. He'd nearly forgotten he was standing in Hannah's front yard for all the world to see.

Though it went against his grain, he let her help him inside the house and even obeyed when she led him to the sofa and commanded him to sit.

"Ham and Swiss or grilled cheese?" she asked.

"Hannah, for crying out loud, I'm not crippled. I can do it myself."

She arched a brow, then reached for the portable phone on the end table beside the sofa and dialed a number.

"Hello, can you connect me with Billy Bishop, please?"

Seth frowned darkly. Dammit, anyway, but this woman was pushy. "Hannah," he warned, "hang up the phone."

She ignored him. "Hi, Billy, this is Hannah Michaels. I've got Seth Granger here and he asked if you could come over."

Seth reached for the phone, but she turned away, so he grabbed her by the waist instead and pulled her down on the sofa beside him.

"He was wondering if you'd like to interview him," she said into the receiver even as he tried to yank it away from her. "Maybe an exposé on the secret life of an Albuquerque cop and the—"

He pinned her beneath him as he nearly lay on her and twisted the phone from her hands. "Listen, Billy," he said, "Hannah wasn't serious, she—"

Seth heard the dial tone and realized there was no one on the other end. He pushed the off button and frowned down at her. Her eyes sparkled with mischief and silky wisps of blond hair tumbled around her flushed face.

He felt the first jolt of desire hit and ripple through him, then indulged himself by breathing in the distinctly feminine scent of her smooth, soft skin.

He should let her go. He knew he should.

He didn't.

"Very funny, Miss Michaels," he said roughly. "I should arrest you for that little stunt."

"Arrest me?" She drew her brows together. "On what grounds?"

"Interfering with an officer during—" he thought for a moment "—ah, the commission of a crime."

"And what crime was that?"

Being too damn sexy, he wanted to say. "Aiding and abetting the enemy."

"Billy Bishop is hardly the enemy, Seth. He's a reporter."

"Same difference."

Hannah laughed at that. The very thought of timid, mild-mannered Billy being anyone's enemy was ludicrous. She started to tell Seth that, but when she looked into his eyes, she completely forgot not only what she was going to say, but she forgot about Billy Bishop, as well. The way Seth was looking at her, she wasn't certain she could remember her own name.

His black eyes glittered as he stared down at her, made her pulse quicken and her skin tighten. The warmth of his body seared her, made her blood rush through her veins and her breath catch in her throat.

This was crazy. Rolling around on her sofa in the middle of the afternoon with a man she barely knew was absolutely insane. She simply didn't do things like this. She had responsibilities, children. Neighbors. She could only imagine what Thelma Goodman across the street would say if she saw what was happening right here in Hannah Michaels's living room.

Hannah knew if she put her hand on Seth's chest or if she simply asked him to get off her, that he would. Knew that she could end this as quickly as it had started.

But she couldn't help herself, couldn't seem to stop what was happening here. She felt more aware of this man than she ever had of any other man. Felt more aware of herself as a woman.

She didn't *want* to stop it.

It felt wonderful. *She* felt wonderful. For just a few minutes, couldn't she just pretend that she was like other women? How long had it been since she'd teased or flirted with a man? Too long, she knew. Much too long.

She told herself that there was no real danger with Seth, that she could control the situation. They were just playing around. Nothing was happening, or would happen, that either one of them would take seriously, for heaven's sake.

So she went with it, let herself enjoy the moment. She touched a finger to his chest and made a circle. "If you're going to arrest me, Officer—"

"Detective."

"If you're going to arrest me, *Detective* Granger," she said, and was startled by the breathless sound of her own voice, "aren't you supposed to read me my rights first?"

"You have the right to remain silent," he said evenly, then moved his hands down her arms and circled her wrists with his fingers as if he'd handcuffed her.

She shuddered at his touch, then pressed her lips firmly together.

"If you give up that right," he continued, "then anything you say can and will be used against you."

He lifted her arms over her head and pinned her to the sofa underneath him. Hannah's heart slammed against her ribs so hard she was certain he could hear.

"If you would like a lawyer..."

His voice trailed off and when his gaze dropped to her mouth, she felt her heart stop. His hands tightened on her wrists as he slowly lowered his head to hers. Anticipation shivered through her.

His lips touched hers gently. He nipped at the corner of her mouth, then her bottom lip. *Kiss me!* she wanted to scream at him, but he seemed intent on taking his time, and she didn't have the courage to actually say it.

His lips teased endlessly, but never made full contact with her mouth. When his tongue swept across her bottom lip, she moaned.

Sensation after sensation shimmered through her, each one more exquisite than the one before. The stubble of his beard rasped across her chin; tremors of electricity coursed through her body. She parted her lips, wanting more, but not quite knowing how to ask.

Finally, blissfully, his lips covered hers fully. His tongue slipped inside her mouth, and she met him eagerly. His taste was heady, hot and masculine. Exciting. Her body felt as if it were on fire; her breasts ached to be touched, not just by his hands, but by his mouth. The thought shocked as much as aroused her.

Impossible, she thought dimly. This is simply not happening. She was certain that it was the middle of the night, that she would wake from this erotic dream any second. Only she didn't want to wake up, she told herself. If this really was a dream, then she wanted to stay asleep, wanted to know, wanted to *feel* what would happen next.

With his hands holding her wrists and his body pressing her into the sofa, she gave herself up completely to his kiss, met every stroke of his tongue with her own, answered every moan, every sigh. And felt more alive than she had in years.

Seth had lost the ability to think. It seemed that all he was capable of at the moment was his overwhelming need to kiss Hannah, to touch her. The attraction had been there from the beginning, so he wasn't surprised. What surprised him was the intensity of the hunger clawing at his insides.

Her slender body underneath his own already had his blood boiling, and those soft little moans coming from deep in her throat were turning him inside out. He'd told himself to keep his distance from this woman, had known instinctively that something like this would happen. But had he listened?

Of course he hadn't.

He lifted his head and looked down at her, at her flushed cheeks and moist, kiss-swollen lips. Her eyelashes fluttered, then opened slowly. He saw the desire there, knew that she was feeling the same thing he was.

So what was the problem? They both understood what happened in the bedroom between a man and a woman. This was about pleasure. Simple, uncomplicated sex between two willing adults. Whenever he'd been with a woman, he'd always been careful. Hannah might be different than any other woman he'd been with before, but he'd be careful with her, too.

So what was the problem?

"Seth?"

The sound of his name on her lips had him lowering his head again. No problem, he told himself. He wanted her. She wanted him. That was as uncomplicated as it got.

He slid his hands down her arms and covered her

mouth with his. She arched upward, pressing herself closer to him—

The muffled ring came from underneath them.

Dammit.

On a heavy sigh, Seth rolled away while Hannah struggled to retrieve the phone that had dropped down between the cushions.

He wasn't certain whether he wanted to strangle whoever was on the other end of the line or thank them. He sat, then slowly released the breath he'd been holding.

"Hello?" Hannah ran a shaky hand through her tousled hair. "I'm sorry, Aunt Martha. No, no, of course I didn't hang up on you yesterday. The line went dead and I wasn't able to call you back. I was walking to the phone this very minute to try calling you again."

Seth raised a brow at Hannah's obvious lie. Hannah glanced at him guiltily, then quickly looked away.

"You're absolutely right, Aunt Martha," she continued. "I should have at least called you from a neighbor's house. I wasn't thinking. Yes, you're absolutely right. It was thoughtless of me."

Seth frowned, already deciding he didn't care much for Hannah's aunt. He could hear the woman's shrill voice from where he was sitting. She sounded like the buzz of a hornet.

Hannah pressed the pause button on her phone and looked at him. "I'm sorry. It's my aunt in Boston. I have to take this. I—uh, well, I—" The sound of her aunt's voice on the phone rose to what sounded like a screech and Hannah released the pause button. "Yes, yes, of course I'm here. I'm sorry. There must be something wrong with my phone."

She turned and walked away. "Nothing happened here. Of course the girls are fine…"

Seth watched Hannah as she disappeared into the kitchen. Obviously Aunt Martha hadn't heard about Maddie's escapade in the tree, or that Hannah had a male houseguest. And obviously Hannah didn't want her aunt to know.

He wondered why, then told himself it was none of his business. Hannah didn't owe him any explanations about her life any more than he owed her any about his.

She was one tempting woman. He could still taste her, still feel the burn of her skin against his own. He wanted her, there was no question about that. But he was thinking clearly now, and after what had just happened between them, he knew it was best to leave things as they were. The last thing he wanted to do was hurt her.

He waited several moments for his pulse to return to normal and the ache in his loins to pass. He could hear her in the kitchen talking with her aunt. He couldn't hear the words, but the conciliatory tone disturbed him.

None of your business, he reminded himself.

With a sigh, he picked up the book he'd attempted to read earlier and forced Ms. Hannah Michaels from his mind.

Five

It took several hours for Hannah to feel back in control again. She'd been relieved to discover that Seth had gone back to his room by the time she'd finished talking to her aunt—correction, *listening* to her aunt—while the woman lectured on manners and common courtesies, and how would Melissa and Madeline ever know how to behave if their own mother couldn't set the proper example for them?

And on and on and on...

Hannah had barely listened to her aunt rant and rave, but she'd known instinctively where to insert the proper, "Yes, Aunt Martha," or "Of course, Aunt Martha," or her aunt's favorite, "You're absolutely right, Aunt Martha."

Hannah hadn't said anything about what had happened with the girls, or that Seth had rescued Maddie from the tree. Her aunt would probably have had an aneurism. Heaven only knew what the woman would do if she found out that Hannah had invited Seth to stay in the house. There was no question she would highly disapprove. Her aunt was rich, demanding, and definitely a prude.

But other than Maddie and Missy, Martha was the only family that Hannah had left, and in spite of the woman's difficult ways and stern tongue, Hannah loved her, knew that in her own way, Martha loved her, too, and only wanted what was best for her and the girls. The problem being that Martha's idea of what was best and Hannah's were completely different.

Hannah could only imagine what her aunt would say if she'd had any idea what she'd interrupted with her phone call: a steamy, bone-melting, tempestuous kiss between her niece and a man who was practically a stranger.

Hannah had been torn between relief and disappointment that her aunt had called. Even now, as she carried a load of dirty clothes to the downstairs laundry room, she wasn't sure how she felt about her...*encounter* with Seth Granger. Her lips still tingled and her stomach still did cartwheels every time she remembered that kiss—which was only every thirty seconds or so.

Maybe she was overreacting, she thought as she stuffed a load of towels into the washer and turned the water on. She and Seth had been joking around. He'd kissed her, and she'd kissed him back. It was perfectly normal for men and women to feel an attraction to each other and test it out a little.

It had just been so long since a man had touched her like that, longer since she'd really wanted one to touch her like that.

She poured liquid soap into the washer and closed

the lid. She wouldn't have let it go much farther than it had, Hannah told herself. She would have stopped him if he'd tried to take it to the next step.

Liar.

She went still at the accusation that popped unwillingly into her brain.

"I would have," she said indignantly.

Hannah Louise Michaels, you're a big fat liar, her subconscious argued. *You know you wanted him to touch you.*

Hannah pressed her lips firmly together and opened the dryer. The clothes inside were still warm and fluffy. She pulled out the black T-shirt Seth had been wearing yesterday and frowned at the rip in the shoulder.

Okay, so maybe she *had* wanted him to touch her. So maybe her breasts had ached and her nipples had hardened. And maybe she'd even felt an ache lower, between her legs. Maybe she'd wanted him to touch her there, too. But wanting something to happen was quite different from actually acting on it.

There was nothing wrong with a little fantasy, she told herself as she folded the T-shirt and laid it on the dryer top. Absolutely nothing wrong with it at all.

Smoothing her fingers over the warm, soft fabric, she let her mind wander once again to that first touch of his lips on hers, the first slide of his tongue into her mouth. The feel of his hands circling her wrists, and the hard press of his body against her own.

The washing machine began its wash cycle: *swish-chug, swish-chug, swish-chug.* The scent of fabric softener and soap hung in the air. It seemed as if all her senses had been heightened since that moment he'd kissed her. Outside, she heard the sounds of Maddie and Missy jumping rope in the backyard and Beau's shrill bark from next door as the animal watched the girls play. Even on her drive to pick the girls up from school this afternoon, Hannah had been more aware of things she saw every day but never really noticed: Bonnie Thurston's mailbox had ivy growing up its post; Lubao Avenue had been repaved; Henry Wilcox, the crossing guard at the school, had grown a mustache.

Hannah pulled Seth's jeans out of the dryer and stared at them. The denim was well worn, faded at the knees and the behind. It had been a long time since she'd washed a man's clothes. It felt strangely intimate to her. She folded them in half, then studied the jagged tear that ran up the left leg.

"You don't have to wash my clothes."

She jumped at the sound of his voice from the doorway, felt her heart leap into her throat. Good grief, but the man had a way of sneaking up on a person! At least she hadn't been dancing or singing to herself this time.

"I do laundry almost every day," she said with a shrug that she hoped appeared relaxed. "It's no big deal. I'm sorry about the hole in your T-shirt and the rip in your jeans. I'll mend them for you tonight."

He frowned. "It's not—"

"Necessary," she finished for him, then smiled. "I know. But I want to do it."

"Hannah, you don't need to. You've done plenty enough for me already."

Her breath caught at his words. She was certain he wasn't referring to the kiss they'd shared earlier, but nonetheless, the kiss was what came to her mind.

"I'm sorry." She quickly turned away from him, laid his jeans on top of the dryer, then reached inside for a pair of Missy's black stretch pants. "I don't mean to be pushy."

Of all the words that might describe Hannah, Seth thought, *pushy* was most certainly not one of them. Based on the blush suddenly sweeping across her face, Seth knew she was thinking about what had happened between them this afternoon. It amazed, as well as intrigued him, that a woman with two children could embarrass as easily as Hannah did.

Even the way she'd kissed him this afternoon had seemed to have an air of innocence about it. Not exactly chaste, but not exactly experienced, either. Those soft lips of hers had tasted warm and sweet and unbelievably arousing.

He watched her busily fold the tiny black pants in her hand. When she reached back into the dryer and pulled out a bath towel, he stepped closer and took hold of her hand. She jerked away from his touch, as if he'd burned her.

"Hannah," he said quietly. "We need to talk about this afternoon."

She held the towel tightly to her. "Okay."

Dammit, couldn't she say something more than okay? He dragged a hand through his hair. "Look, it just sort of happened, then before we knew it, it probably got a little out of hand. I didn't mean to scare you, or freak you out."

"You didn't...freak me out."

Well, she certainly *looked* freaked out, he thought irritably. Her eyes were wide, her voice strained, and she was clutching that damn blue towel as if it were a shield.

"If it's awkward for me to be here now, just say so and I'll get a room at the motel in town."

She shook her head. "I just...it's only...what I mean

is—" She closed her eyes. "I've never done anything like that before."

"What?" He furrowed his brow. "You've never kissed a man before?"

"Of course I've kissed a man before," she said with exasperation. "I do have children, for heaven's sake. I mean I've never kissed a strange man like that before."

"How do you usually kiss strange men?"

His teasing seemed to relax her, and the smile she gave him was sweet and beguiling and made his chest hitch.

"I mean I've never kissed a man I didn't know well." She glanced at the towel in her hands. "I'm a little embarrassed at what you must think of me."

"I don't think anything of you," he said, then added when she looked up at him, "For God's sake, that didn't come out the way I meant it. Hannah, I kissed you. You kissed me back. It was terrific. But we both know it's not going anywhere."

"It's not?"

His heart slammed against his ribs at her comment. He watched the blush on her cheeks deepen.

"I mean, it's not," she said quickly. "Of course it's not."

"I'm only going to be here a few days," he said carefully, "but I promise I won't touch you again."

She looked down at the towel in her hand. "Okay."

"Unless—" He saw Hannah draw in a breath as he reached across her and picked up his clothes.

She lifted her eyes and stared at him. "Unless what?"

"Unless you ask me to."

"Oh."

When he straightened and stepped back, she released the breath she'd been holding.

He was at the doorway when she called to him.

"Seth?"

He glanced over his shoulder.

"You were obviously on your way somewhere, before all this happened. I should have asked you if I can do anything for you. Call someone, maybe, or—"

"I'm fine." It was much too complicated to explain, and it wasn't something he cared to talk about, anyway. "I have an appointment in Wolf River, but it can keep."

"I could drive you," she offered. "Lori would watch the girls for me and I could—"

"I've already called. You don't have to do a thing."

"But if it's important," she persisted, "if you need to meet someone, then I'll take you."

If you need to meet someone.

His pulse jumped as an image popped into his mind: little Lizzie with her big blue eyes and dark, silky hair; Rand, taller, bigger, his black hair and dark eyes so like Seth's that everyone knew instinctively they were brothers.

"Hannah, stop." He thought of the twenty-three years he'd been separated from his sister and brother. Twenty-three years he'd thought them dead. "Look, I won't lie and tell you it wasn't important. But I've got it handled and a few days won't make a big difference."

"Oh, Seth." She closed her eyes on a sigh. "I'm so sorry."

"It happened, Hannah." He shrugged, then smiled at her. "Besides, I just caught the whiff of something incredible coming from your kitchen. I hope I'm invited."

She smiled back. "I hope meat loaf is all right. I could make you something else if—"

"I love meat loaf." He couldn't remember the last time he'd had a sit-down, home-cooked meal, and the smells were making his mouth water already. "I'll go wash up."

Clean clothes in his arm, he went back to his room and took a shower. As he stood under the spray, the words he'd said kept playing over and over in his head: *a few days won't matter one way or the other.*

He thought of the way she'd felt underneath him today, the perfect fit of her mouth to his, the instantaneous combustion in his blood when she'd so eagerly kissed him back.

He turned the water to cold and began to wonder if living in this house with Hannah, even for a few days, might indeed make a difference, after all.

"Derek Matthews can burp the alphabet all the way up to *G*," Maddie announced first thing at the dinner table that evening.

"Is that so?" Hannah scooped a spoonful of mashed potatoes onto Maddie's plate first, then Missy's.

"He says he's gonna practice a whole bunch and by next week he'll make it all the way to *Z*," Missy added. "Practice makes perfect, Derek says."

"Did he now?" Hannah glanced up at Seth and saw the amusement in his eyes as he glanced from Maddie to Missy. She'd served him his food first and told him to start eating, but he was waiting politely until everyone at the table had their food.

Hannah reached for the bowl of broccoli on the dining-room table and gave each of her girls a small serving. "Isn't Derek the one who had to go to the nurse two weeks ago because he stuck a bead up his nose?"

Maddie's blond curls danced with excitement as she

nodded. "He said he could blow it five feet up in the air right out of his nostril."

"It was a big yellow one," Missy said, her eyes wide with admiration.

Hannah wasn't certain that Derek's amazing talents were the proper dinner conversation in front of a guest, but she was thankful that her daughters were in their usual chatterbox mode. It seemed to Hannah that every time she opened her mouth around Seth, the wrong thing came out.

She still couldn't believe the words that had come out of her mouth after he'd told her that nothing was going to happen between them. *It's not?* she'd said. Not as a statement, but as a question.

And if it wasn't bad enough she'd said it, did she have to sound so disappointed, too?

She looked at him now, watched as his gaze bounced back and forth between Missy and Maddie as they explained to Seth, in explicit detail, Derek Matthews's bead-in-the-nose incident. Both girls were trying to out-talk the other and it was obvious to Hannah that her daughters were vying for his attention. Except for Lori's husband, John, there'd been no male presence in Maddie's and Missy's lives since their father had left three years ago. Brent had complained that he was too busy, made weak attempts at coming over, but they both knew the truth. He'd never wanted to be a father, and after the twins had been born, he hadn't wanted to be a husband, either.

Seth was the first man that had ever stayed in their house, and the girls were excited that a real-life hero was staying with them.

And the truth be told, *she* was enjoying Seth's company, as well.

She'd heard the water running while she'd made dinner, had tried not to think about him taking a shower, though her mind had definitely wandered. His damp, dark hair was slicked back from his freshly shaven face, and he'd changed into a white T-shirt and clean blue jeans. He'd removed the bandage over his eyebrow, and though there was a bruise, the cut didn't seem as bad today. He'd said little since he'd sat down, but those eyes of his, those dark, watchful eyes, seemed to take everything in.

And she was taking in her own share, Hannah thought as she stared at Seth.

The T-shirt stretched across his broad chest; the sleeves fit snugly over the thick, corded muscles of his bronzed arms. His hands were large and callused and, though she tried not to think about what those hands would feel like on her bare skin, her mind seemed determined to have a will of its own.

She forced herself to stop fantasizing about the man sitting across from her and turned her attention back to Missy and Maddie, who were on the edges of an argument about something.

"Show-and-tell is Friday at nine," Maddie said emphatically.

"No, it's not," Missy insisted. "It's ten."

"Is too."

"Is not."

"Is *too*."

"That's enough, girls," Hannah said with a warning tone. "Ask Miss Reynolds tomorrow. What are you taking this time?"

"We're taking Mr. Granger."

Seth made a strange, choking sound at the other end

of the table. Hannah went very still and stared at her daughters.

"*What* did you say?" she asked.

"All the kids wanna see him," Maddie said. "So Missy and I agreed it would be cool to take him."

Hannah glanced at Seth, saw the fleeting glimpse of sheer terror in his eyes. It seemed that Seth Granger, a man who flew through the air and could leap tall buildings in a single bound, was afraid of children. He looked sharply at her, his gaze imploring her to help him out here.

She tried not to smile, but even as she gave her daughters her most serious look, Hannah felt the corner of her mouth quiver. "I'm afraid you can't take Mr. Granger to show-and-tell, girls."

"Why not?"

"Well…" Hannah had to think a moment. "Just because."

Maddie looked at Seth. "Don't you like kids?"

"Ah…sure," he said hesitantly.

"So can you come?" Missy and Maddie asked at the same time.

"I really don't think I'd be very interesting," Seth said.

"Sure you would. Chelsea brought her uncle one time and he juggled for us." Missy stuck a bite of broccoli in her mouth. "He only dropped the balls once."

"Travis Jeffers brought his hamster last week," Maddie added, then looked at Seth. "You'd be much better than a hamster."

"Thanks," Seth said, his expression flat.

"Don't you wanna come?" Maddie asked Seth.

"Well, I—" He squirmed, then looked at Hannah again.

"Sorry, girls." Hannah shook her head. "You're going to have to think of something else."

"Oookaay," Maddie dragged the word out dramatically while she poked at the potatoes on her plate. "But all the kids at school are gonna be disappointed."

"Maybe we could take the lightning globe Aunt Lori gave us," Missy suggested. "That's pretty cool."

While the girls discussed other options for show-and-tell, Hannah could see that Seth was having a difficult time following their rapid-fire exchange of ideas. Clearly, the man was out of his element.

And what *was* his element? she wondered. She didn't want to pry, and she wouldn't, but there were so many questions bouncing around inside her brain. Questions that were none of her business, but that didn't make her any less curious. The expression on his face when she'd asked him where he'd been going before the accident had been…cautious, she decided was the best word. He'd offered no other explanation than to say he'd been on his way to Wolf River, and that it had been important.

But she was certain she'd seen something in his eyes before he'd answered. A fierce flash of emotion that was gone as quickly as it appeared.

Had he been on his way to meet a woman? For all she knew, he had been on his way to get married. There could be two hundred people waiting right now for him to show up and say, "I do."

Frowning, she stabbed a bite of meat loaf. Well, he certainly shouldn't be kissing her if he was getting married, the jerk. He shouldn't be sitting here, and he shouldn't be—

The sound of her daughters arguing pulled Hannah out of her thoughts.

"Do too!" Maddie said.

"Do not!" Missy fired back.

Good Lord. Hannah sighed. What was it this time?

"You have broccoli in your teeth," Maddie said in a singsong voice.

"I do *not!*"

Maddie picked up a little tree of broccoli and stuck the tiny trunk under her top lip. "Look, I'm Missy," Maddie teased. "I have broccoli growing out of my mouth."

Missy's face turned red with fury. "I'm gonna tell everyone at school you sleep with a blankie!"

"Stop this right now!" Hannah said firmly. "This is no way to behave at the dinner table, especially in front of a guest. Madeline Nicole, you apologize to your sister right now, then to Mr. Granger."

"Sorry." Maddie cast her eyes down.

"Now upstairs, both of you. Obviously, you need a time-out. I'll be up in a minute."

Heads down, both girls left the table. Hannah closed her eyes and sighed heavily. "I'm so sorry. I can't imagine what's gotten into them lately. It seems like every time I turn around, they're misbehaving."

"So you mean they're normal?"

Hannah opened her eyes, saw the smile on Seth's lips. "I don't condone that kind of behavior."

"You might not condone it," he said with a shrug, "but you can't always stop it, either."

She narrowed a gaze at him, wondered if she'd been wrong in her presumptions about him. "You have children?"

"Good God, no." He shook his head. "But I remember my mom sending me and my brother away from the table on more than one occasion."

"You have a brother?"

"Yeah." The look in his eyes was distant. "And a sister."

"Where do they live?" she asked.

He looked at her, then shook his head. "I don't know."

Her brow furrowed with confusion. "You don't know?"

"It's complicated," he said tightly, then tossed his napkin on the table. "Let me help you clean up."

"No, please," she said, still stunned by his statement. "I'm fine here."

He wanted to argue, Hannah could see it in his expression, but he relented. "Thanks for dinner. You make a mean meat loaf."

She smiled. "I take it that's a compliment."

"Yeah." He smiled back and stood. "That's a compliment."

She watched him limp from the room, stared after him for several seconds. He was an enigma, she thought. A confusing, complex man with a past that appeared to weigh heavily on those broad shoulders of his.

She heard the sound of her daughters laughing upstairs and was at least thankful they'd made up. She'd start their bath and then do the dishes, she decided. After that, she had a half-dozen pillows to personalize with hand-stitching, and she had to get up an hour early to start those muffins tomorrow.

As tempting as Seth was, as much as she found herself attracted to him, Hannah didn't have time, or room, in her life for anyone or anything else.

Six

The following afternoon Seth stepped out onto Hannah's front porch. It was a nice day with blue skies, a few puffy white clouds and the slightest hint of fall in the air. Leaves were just beginning to drop onto the neatly mown lawns, and the scent of late-blooming pink roses in Hannah's front yard drifted on the warm breeze. He stopped and listened, was amazed at the quiet. No low-flying planes or helicopters, no buzz of construction saws, no freeway noise or police sirens. He hadn't known a place this quiet existed, wasn't even certain he liked it.

At least his leg felt better today. He was able to walk more easily and the swelling had gone down considerably. Now if only he could get some feedback on the condition of his motorcycle, Seth thought irritably. Hannah's phone had been ringing all morning, but not one call had been from the repair shop. Seth was trying not to lose his temper, but patience had never been his strong suit.

At the sound of a loud, enthusiastic bark, he turned and saw Beau standing on the short picket fence between his yard and Hannah's. The dog's tail thumped back and forth happily, and he barked again.

"So we're buds now, are we?" Seth grinned and limped over to give the big, black shepherd a scratch between his ears. Beau sniffed greedily at Seth's hand.

"Apple spice," Seth told the animal. "Hannah made enough muffins this morning to feed a small country."

Beau barked twice in response.

"Don't I know it," Seth said with a shake of his head. "The woman never stops. Lord only knows what time she went to bed last night and she's upstairs now doing God knows what in that bedroom she's been working on."

Beau cocked his head and gave a short *woof!*

"Hey, pal, I offered to help," Seth defended himself. "But the woman gives new meaning to the word *stubborn.*"

She also gave new meaning to the words *sexy, tenacious* and *tempting,* he thought.

Especially *tempting.*

He hadn't slept well last night thinking about how damn tempting the woman was. The taste of her had lingered in his mouth; her scent, a faint, feminine fragrance, was everywhere. He certainly hadn't meant for that kiss to get out of hand yesterday, but it had. He simply hadn't been thinking. Not with his brain, anyway.

He'd promised not to touch her again—unless she asked him to. He smiled as he remembered the look in her eyes when he'd said that to her in the laundry room yesterday. Her expression had been one of stunned surprise, as if it would never occur to her that she would actually ask a man to touch her.

Seth would stand by his promise, but it wasn't going to be easy. It no longer seemed to matter what was logical or the best thing to do, or even the right thing to do. All she had to do was walk in the room and he knew he wanted her.

Beau whined and Seth frowned at the dog. "Hey, did I say I was going to do anything about it? I can control myself. I'm not an animal, you know."

Beau seemed to agree. He barked happily, then raced away. Seth grinned at the dog's antics, was about to turn away when Beau raced back with a newspaper between his teeth. The dog's large paws hung over the fence as he jumped up and dropped the folded paper at Seth's feet.

"Thanks, pal." Seth patted the dog's head and picked up the paper.

Maybe he would sit on the front porch and read for a while, he decided, though he couldn't imagine there was much to report in the sleepy little town of Ridgewater. He'd return the paper when he finished, then he'd call the motorcycle shop again to find out when the hell his bike would be repaired.

He started up the stairs and opened the paper. Then after he'd made that call, maybe he'd just sort of wander upstairs and see what Hannah was—

HERO POLICE OFFICER FROM ALBUQUERQUE SAVES LITTLE GIRL FROM CERTAIN HARM

The headline stared back at him, as did the quarter-page picture of himself. It wasn't a recent picture, Seth realized, it was his academy graduation picture.

What the *hell?*

Swearing hotly under his breath, he read the first few lines:

In a dramatic and daring rescue late Tuesday afternoon, Detective Seth Granger of the Albuquerque police department crashed his motorcycle through a wooden fence and swiftly climbed a tree in order to save the life of five-year-old Madeline Michaels. Eyewitnesses—

Eyewitnesses? What eyewitnesses! Seth clenched his teeth and kept reading.

—eyewitnesses say that little Maddie, caught on the jagged limb by the pocket of her blue denim pants, had dangled perilously high above the ground and would certainly have sustained serious injury if not for the quick-thinking heroics of Detective Granger.
  Maddie, along with her sister Missy, had been playing…

The article went on in a long, detailed, highly elaborate exaggeration of the entire incident, taking up all of the first page and three-quarters of page two, complete with pictures of people being interviewed and what appeared to be Maddie's and Missy's school pictures.

Seth snapped the paper shut and stomped up the porch steps. Pain radiated up his left leg, and he didn't give a damn.

Billy Bishop was going to die.

Sanding block in her hand, Hannah stood on the top rung of the stepladder and worked at smoothing down the repaired crack over the bedroom window. A fine layer of spackle powder covered her bare arms, blue denim overalls and black tank top. She'd pulled on a Rangers baseball cap, but no doubt a fair amount of the gritty dust had found its way into her ponytail. As soon as she finished sanding this last crack, she was headed for a shower. Between the dust, the dirt and the drops of sweat she could feel sliding down her stomach, Lord knew she needed one.

She fantasized about a bath, with fluffy white clouds of strawberry-scented bubbles. She could picture several votives flickering while she soaked in the warm water, her head resting on the rim of the tub, her eyes closed while she listened to something Celtic, like Loreena McKennitt, or maybe something romantic, like Andrea Bocelli. She could hear the tenor's velvety voice now, the incredible, soothing tone of his rich, deep—

"Hannah!"

Startled at the sudden bellow of her name, she wobbled on the ladder, barely catching herself before she fell.

"Hannah!" Seth came barreling through the doorway of the bedroom, a newspaper in his hand. "Have you *seen* this?"

Oh, dear.

"Have you?" he asked impatiently.

"The newspaper?"

"Yes," he said tightly and moved beside the step-ladder. He frowned up at her. "*Today's* newspaper."

"No, I haven't seen it."

Which was true. She didn't subscribe to the *Gazette* because not only didn't she have the extra money, she didn't have the time to read the paper. Besides, in a town as small as Ridgewater, she'd hear about anything newsworthy soon enough.

But she'd certainly *heard* plenty about the article. The phone had been ringing all morning. And since Seth had made it clear from the beginning that he hadn't wanted any media attention, Hannah had avoided mentioning anything to him about the article.

Somehow, though, he'd gotten his hands on a copy.

"Front page," he said with something close to a snarl and thrust the paper under her nose. "The front, flipping page!"

She looked at the paper. Good heavens, Seth's picture took up nearly half the page. "Ah, that's a very nice photograph."

"Hannah." He closed his eyes on a swear word, then drew in a slow breath. "Come down here."

She didn't want to. Not because she was afraid of him because he was angry, but because she felt so much more confident high up on the ladder, towering over him. "I really have to finish this sanding, and then I have to—"

"Please." There was more starch in that single word than in a preacher's collar.

Still holding the sanding block, she stepped down the ladder until she was eye-to-eye with him.

"Hannah." His narrowed gaze held hers. "I'm an undercover cop."

"An undercover cop?" she repeated.

"Yeah." He took the sanding block from her hand and set it on the ladder step. "And what do you think would be the last thing an undercover cop would want anyone to know?"

She swallowed. "That's he's an undercover cop?"

"Right."

An undercover cop. Dear Lord. "Seth, I'm so sorry. I had no idea."

"That's the general idea." He glared at the picture of himself.

A sudden thought made her breath catch in her throat. "You aren't, I mean, you coming here, to Ridgewater—"

"On an assignment? Here?" He lifted one brow and tilted his head. "No, Hannah. I'm not working right now."

She supposed it was a ridiculous question, but she felt better to hear him say it, anyway. "You're on vacation?"

"Not exactly. I'm on a...what did you call it last night?" He thought for a moment. "Oh, yeah. A time-out."

"A time-out?"

"I had a disagreement with my boss. I don't like his policies, and he doesn't approve of what he calls my 'insubordination.'"

"He gave you a time-out for insubordination?"

"Actually, I'm on forced leave for punching the bastard in the nose."

"You punched your boss in the nose?" She felt like an idiot, either repeating everything he said, or answering him with a question. "Why?"

"He refused backup at the last bust I was involved in, said it wasn't necessary. It nearly got my partner killed, not to mention the uniformed cop who stumbled into the operation at a very unfortunate moment. It's a miracle no one died. By the time Jarris showed up on the scene, I was...perturbed."

Jarris. Seth had uttered that name after he'd fallen out of the tree. "So you punched him—Jarris."

Satisfaction glinted in Seth's dark eyes. "Yeah. I punched him."

"And you're on forced leave for how long?"

"Six weeks."

"Six weeks! Good heavens, and my girls think fifteen minutes is a long time."

He almost smiled at that, then stared at the paper again. "Six weeks will be nothing compared to what Jarris will do if he sees this. I'll either end up at a desk filling out forms, or wearing white gloves directing traffic somewhere."

"Oh, Seth, I'm so sorry." Hannah sighed. "No doubt you've noticed by now, but not much ever happens in Ridgewater."

He looked at her as if she'd just made the understatement of the century, but he didn't say anything.

"This story," she went on, "as simple and as unimportant as it might seem to you, was like a big, meaty bone to Billy. If he'd known, I'm sure he never would have run this article."

"He's a reporter, Hannah." He tossed the newspaper on the floor. "That's what reporters do. They can't help themselves."

She supposed he was right. Billy probably would have run the article anyway, but she was certain he wouldn't have run the picture. She glanced up sharply at that thought. "Does this put you in any danger?"

He shook his head. "I doubt it. This picture is old enough, and after my last assignment, Jarris probably won't use me for deep cover anymore."

"Why not?"

"Well, this might surprise you," he said evenly, "but he seems to think I don't follow orders very well."

Hannah widened her eyes. "No."

"Hard to believe, I know." He shrugged, then leaned closer, as if he were going to tell her a secret. "He also thinks I have a bad attitude."

"Really?" The warmth of his breath on her ear made Hannah shiver. "Why would he possibly think that?"

"I like to do things my own way," he said. "In my own time."

She swallowed, heard the sound of her pulse beating in her head. Felt the quickening of her blood. "Is that so?"

"Yeah." He didn't touch her, but he moved into her, put his hands on the ladder, enclosing her on the first step where she stood. "He says I'm too unpredictable. Too impulsive."

Hannah couldn't believe she was having this conversation with Seth. She couldn't believe that she was standing here on this ladder, covered with dust and dirt, no makeup and her hair a mess, and yet, with the way Seth was looking at her, she felt…sexy.

"So are you?" she asked breathlessly.

"Am I what?"

Hannah held her breath as his gaze wandered over her face, then settled on her mouth. Her heart beat like a drum, heavy and hollow, fast.

"Impulsive."

"No."

She felt a stab of disappointment. "Oh."

"I always know exactly what I'm doing," he murmured. "And I know exactly what I want. Do you?"

She couldn't concentrate with his body so close to hers; she couldn't think. But she managed to shake her head.

He stared at her mouth; she thought for certain he would kiss her. She *wanted* him to kiss her!

He straightened suddenly, then dropped his hands from the ladder and turned away. The disappointment she'd felt only a moment ago turned to sheer frustration.

She realized she *did* know what she wanted, but she didn't know how to ask. Didn't have a clue what the words were; was certain she couldn't say them if she did know. She was grateful he kept his back to her while he glanced around the room. She needed a moment to gather her wits, to compose herself.

He wasn't limping as badly today, Hannah noticed as she watched him walk to the window, then move to the doorway leading to the bathroom. "How's your leg?"

"Better." He ran his hand over a crack she'd already repaired by the doorway. "You do nice work."

"Thanks." Needing something to hold on to, she picked up the sanding block he'd taken out of her hands a few minutes ago. "I only have one more bedroom to finish after this one."

He poked his head in the bathroom. She'd bought new white-and-black tiles for the floor and around the existing tub, but she hadn't the money to pay anyone to set them yet.

He knelt and looked at the boxed brass ceiling fan Hannah had bought on a closeout from the hardware store. "For your bed-and-breakfast?"

She nodded. "I hope to be open by Christmas."

"So what's stopping you?"

She really didn't care to discuss her financial situation with Seth. The last thing she wanted from him was pity or sympathy. "My grandparents left this house to my mother and my aunt Martha. When my mom passed away six years ago, the house became half mine. It was rented out until the girls and I moved in three years ago, after—"

When she paused, he glanced up. "After your divorce?"

"Separation," she said, then climbed back up the ladder and rubbed the sanding block over the spackle. "The divorce wasn't final for another year after that."

He'd ask now, she thought. People always wanted to know what happened and why. It shouldn't bother her, she knew. What difference should it make now? And in her heart, she knew that both she and the girls were better off because of it.

But the fact was, it did bother her. And with Seth, even more so.

"So this aunt of yours," he said, "does she live in Ridgewater?"

Hannah slowly released the breath she'd been holding. He hadn't asked, she thought with relief, and felt the tension ease from her shoulders.

"She was raised here, but she got married and moved to Boston when I was a little girl."

"She wasn't happy with you yesterday, was she?" he asked. "When she called."

Once again, the memory of Seth's kiss flooded her senses. Hannah bit the inside of her mouth, forced the feelings and the image from her mind. With a shrug, she blew at the dust on the wall. "She's been lonely since my uncle died a couple of years ago, but she keeps busy with the Cambridge Revolutionary Society, and she's president of the Boston Women's Cultural League."

At the two short blasts from a car's horn, Hannah climbed down the ladder and glanced out the window. Maddie and Missy had just jumped out of Lori's big black Yukon and were running up the front walk.

"Up here," Hannah yelled down when she heard the front door slam open.

"Mommy! Mommy!" the girls both called to her at the same time as they pounded up the stairs. "We're famous!"

Hannah looked apologetically at Seth, who simply folded his arms and leaned back against the wall.

Maddie and Missy bounded into the room and ran to her. "Look, Mommy, look!" Maddie said as she waved the newspaper around. "Me and Missy got our pictures in the paper!"

"Missy and I," Hannah corrected her daughter.

"No, not you. Just Missy and me," Maddie said excitedly, then ran to Seth. "And you, Mr. Granger. Look at this. You're on the front page and everything!"

"How 'bout that?" Seth knelt and glanced at the picture as if he'd never seen it before. The wince in his eyes was barely noticeable, Hannah thought.

Hannah appreciated the smile Seth gave her daughters, though she was certain it took tremendous effort on his part. She watched her daughters jumping up and down with excitement as they pointed to their pictures and told Seth how their teacher had asked them both to come up and tell the class what had happened. The paper had even mentioned the girls' birthday in a couple of weeks, which delighted them both to no end. When he bent down to their level, Maddie and Missy put their hands on Seth's shoulders and leaned against him, would have climbed in his lap if they could have.

It amazed Hannah how easily her daughters had accepted Seth. Over the past year, Hannah had gone out on an occasional date, usually when Lori or one of the other well-meaning women in Ridgewater had set her up with an eligible bachelor. And though all her dates had been extremely friendly to both her daughters, neither Maddie or Missy had ever warmed up to even one of the men.

But then neither had she, Hannah noted.

Of all the men to "warm up" to, Hannah thought with a sigh, Seth Granger was the worse possible choice. For her and her daughters.

"Girls." Hannah set the sanding block down and reached for a rag to wipe off her hands. "Go wash your hands and I'll be down in a minute to make you a snack."

"Okay," they both said at the same time. Maddie grabbed one of Seth's hands, Missy, the other. "Can you have a snack with us, Mr. Granger?"

Hannah saw the hesitation in Seth's eyes, but the girls didn't give him a chance to answer. They tugged him toward the doorway, chattering the entire time about the newspaper article. She saw him glance over his shoulder, a look of bewilderment on his face, and couldn't help but smile at him when Maddie asked if he liked peanut butter and bananas on toast.

Maddie and Missy stopped abruptly at the doorway and turned. "Oh, Aunt Lori said to tell you that we're leaving for camp at three tomorrow instead of four 'cause the dentist cancelled her appointment."

Before Hannah could say anything, they were gone, like two dancing bubbles of pure energy.

Camp? What camp?

Hannah felt her heart skip as she remembered. *Camp Wickamackee.* With everything that had happened this week, she'd forgotten that Lori was taking Maddie and Missy to weekend camp at the lake. Lori had been a counselor there for ten years and she'd taken the girls twice a year since they were three.

She heard the sound of her daughters' laughing, then the splash of running water from the bathroom.

Alone.

She stared blindly at the rag in her hand, then drew in a long, slow breath.

She and Seth were going to be alone this weekend.

Seven

"Ten days! You've got to be kidding. What could possibly take ten days!"

Teeth clenched, Seth listened while Ned Morgan, from Morgan's Frame and Auto Body, explained the damage that had been done to Seth's motorcycle and the estimate. The parts were on back order and would be shipped from California in four days, Ned told Seth, then said that he and his son, Ed, would be "fixing" to start disassembly right away.

Ned and Ed. Terrific.

Just terrific.

Seth hung up the phone in Hannah's living room and swore for five minutes straight.

He'd already been here five days, now he was looking at another ten. He knew he wasn't ready to get back on his motorcycle just yet; his ankle was still swollen, and if he put too much pressure on it, little rockets of pain shot through his leg. But ten days! He dragged a hand through his hair and groaned. He couldn't stay here that long.

Dammit, he *couldn't*.

At the sound of Beau's excited barking, Seth grabbed a wrapped chocolate mint from a crystal bowl on the coffee table and moved to the window. He looked out as Hannah pulled her minivan into the driveway. He unwrapped the mint and popped it in his mouth, watched her park, then slide out of her front seat and greet the dog.

She'd made herself scarce since Maddie and Missy had left yesterday to go to camp with Lori and her family. After she'd cooked him that awesome dinner last night—chicken with some kind of herbs, little red potatoes and peas—she'd put on a wine-colored sheath dress, clipped her hair up on her head, then said goodbye at around seven and told him to enjoy the quiet. She hadn't come home until after midnight.

Midnight, for crying out loud.

Today, she'd left the house around eleven, dressed in a long yellow floral skirt and white tank top with a matching short-sleeved sweater. He was used to seeing her in jeans and overalls, and he couldn't help but wonder what she'd gotten all dressed up for.

Or *who.*

He wouldn't ask, though. It certainly wasn't any of *his* business. Why wouldn't she go out? Her daughters were away for the weekend. With two five-year-olds, he supposed she didn't have an opportunity to get out of the house and have fun very often. It wasn't like she had to hang around just because he was here.

There hadn't been any guys at the house since he'd been here, but Seth had no doubts there were more than a few single men sniffing around. Hannah was a beautiful woman, intelligent, sexy. When she smiled, she went from beautiful to dazzling.

She was smiling now, talking to Beau and petting the big dog's head. He felt a tug in his chest as he watched her, a strange longing that tightened at the sound of her laugh.

Lust, he told himself. Plain and simple lust.

He might have a sore ankle, but the rest of his body was working just fine. After he'd heard Hannah come in last night, he'd spent the next two hours tossing and turning, thinking about her, imagined her taking off that pretty little dress she had on, then sliding off her bra and pulling on her short nightgown. He'd seen her legs under that nightgown, long and curvy, made to wrap around a man's waist. That thought, and the realization that her bedroom was directly over his, that she was alone upstairs in her bed, was enough to make him break out in a sweat. It had taken him another hour after that before he'd finally fallen asleep.

He was truly beginning to regret the fact he'd promised not to touch her. Two days ago, when she'd been on that ladder and he'd moved in so close to her, he'd nearly broken that promise. It had taken every ounce of willpower he possessed not to kiss her the way he'd wanted, not to unbuckle the overalls she had on and cup her breasts in his hands, then take the tip of each soft mound in his mouth and taste her there.

Just thinking about that made his pulse quicken and his blood heat up. He'd wanted her naked and underneath him so badly he'd ached. He ached now, dammit. He watched that pretty skirt flow around those long legs of hers and wondered how many buttons he'd have to

If offer card is missing write to: Silhouette Reader Service, 3010 Walden Ave., P.O. Box 1867, Buffalo NY 14240-1867

NO POSTAGE
NECESSARY
IF MAILED
IN THE
UNITED STATES

BUSINESS REPLY MAIL

FIRST-CLASS MAIL   PERMIT NO. 717-003   BUFFALO, NY

POSTAGE WILL BE PAID BY ADDRESSEE

SILHOUETTE READER SERVICE
3010 WALDEN AVE
PO BOX 1867
BUFFALO NY 14240-9952

Do You Have the LUCKY KEY?

PLAY THE Lucky Key Game

and you can get

FREE BOOKS and a FREE GIFT!

Scratch the gold areas with a coin. Then check below to see the books and gift you can get!

YES! I have scratched off the gold areas. Please send me the 2 FREE BOOKS and GIFT for which I qualify. I understand I am under no obligation to purchase any books, as explained on the back of this card.

326 SDL DNVG   225 SDL DNVC

FIRST NAME   LAST NAME

ADDRESS

APT.#   CITY

STATE/PROV.   ZIP/POSTAL CODE

🔑🔑🔑🔑 2 free books plus a free gift   🔑🔑🔑🔑 1 free book

🔑🔑🔑🔑 2 free books   🔑🔑🔑🔑 Try Again!

Visit us online at www.eHarlequin.com

Offer limited to one per household and not valid to current Silhouette Desire® subscribers. All orders subject to approval.

undo before it slid down over her hips, and what it would feel like to—

Stop, he told himself. If he went any further with this line of thinking, he would most likely embarrass himself when Hannah walked in the house.

He moved away from the window, heard the back door off the laundry room open, then Hannah's soft humming as she entered the living room with a small wrapped brown package in one arm. He watched her slip her black shoulder purse onto the sofa end table, then turn and stare at the hallway which led to his bedroom. She stood there for a long moment, a thoughtful look on her face, took a step toward the hall. She stopped, bit her bottom lip, then shook her head.

When she turned back around and saw him, she jumped back.

"Seth!" She slapped a hand to her chest. "You startled me."

"Sorry." Was she heading for his bedroom when she'd obviously thought better of it? "You look nice."

"What? Oh." Her eyelashes fluttered down, and she smoothed a hand over her skirt. "Thank you."

She looked tired, he thought, and once again found himself wondering exactly what she'd been doing last night and today, and who she'd been doing it with.

It's none of your business.

"Your phone rang several times today," he said, deciding to stay in neutral conversational territory. "And the mailman had me sign for a letter. I set it on the coffee table."

She glanced at the letter, then stepped to the table and picked it up. A smile touched the corners of her mouth as she gripped the letter tightly to her. "Thank you."

He wasn't certain whether she was thanking him or a higher deity, but the relief on her face was evident. The letter was obviously one she'd been waiting for.

"I'll make some dinner," she said, turning as she opened the letter. "I might even have a bottle of wine in the—"

She had her back to him when she stopped abruptly at the kitchen door and stared at the letter.

"Something wrong?"

When she didn't answer, just stood there, her back perfectly straight and her shoulders stiff, he moved toward her.

"What's wrong, Hannah?"

"I—he—" She looked up, her expression of relief was gone now, in its place a look of confusion. She closed her eyes, opened them again, then quickly stuffed the letter back into the envelope. "Nothing's wrong. I've got some steaks and baked potatoes for tonight. I hope that's all right. I'll just throw a salad together and—"

"Hannah." He moved into the dining room. "Tell me what's wrong."

"Everything is fine, Seth. Really." She smiled tightly at him. "It's been a long day, that's all. If you wouldn't mind, I'd just like a few minutes by myself."

He watched her disappear into the kitchen. He wouldn't follow her, dammit. She'd made it clear she wanted to be alone. He'd respect that. Give her some space.

He listened for some kind of sound from the kitchen, but there was nothing. Absolute quiet.

None of your business, he reminded himself again, then went out onto the front porch and stared at the sun as it slowly sank into the horizon.

* * *

Hannah stood at the kitchen counter and stared at the crisp, white envelope in her hand. The paper burned her fingers; heat radiated up her arm and through her body. He hadn't even called, hadn't had the nerve to prepare her for this.

Her hand shook as she pulled the check from her ex-husband out of the envelope. The amount blurred in front of her eyes: one hundred and fifty dollars.

She stared at the figure, praying another zero would magically appear so the number would be just a little bit closer to what it was supposed to be. The number she needed to pay her aunt the three months rent she was behind; the number she needed to pay the electric bill due now; the number she needed to make the credit-card payment that was already one month late.

But the number, like Brent, would never change. She'd been a fool and an idiot to think it would. He'd done this for the past three years, promised her he'd be on time, promised her that the amount would be correct. But it never was. Last week, when she'd threatened to take further action, he'd assured her that a real-estate deal had finally closed and he would make up for the past few months he'd missed.

Sure he would, she thought and stared at the check again. When pigs fly.

She bit her lip and blinked furiously. She wouldn't cry, darn it.

She *wouldn't.*

If she could, she'd shred the check, grind it up in the garbage disposal and wash it down the drain. For that one moment, at least, she'd feel better.

But the moment would pass quickly, she knew, and the fact was, one hundred and fifty dollars was better than nothing. Not much, she thought miserably, but it would put a few groceries on the table, at least, and maybe pay the electric bill.

Tossing the letter aside, Hannah closed her eyes when she felt the burn of tears. *"Damn you, Brent Michaels,"* she said, gripping the kitchen counter.

A lump rose in her throat; she did her best to swallow it back. She wouldn't think about this now, she told herself. She was too emotional at the moment. If she kept busy, she'd be all right. She needed to wash the potatoes, chop up some carrots...

The first tear slid down her cheek and splashed on the white tile. Furious with herself, she wiped at her face, but it did no good. That single tear had opened a floodgate she couldn't seem to close.

Oh, what the hell.

With a sob, she dropped her face into her hands and did something she never allowed herself to do.

She cried.

Seth found her like that two minutes later. Standing at the counter, with her head in her hands, her shoulders racked with sobs. He nearly walked back out of the kitchen. She'd asked to be alone, hadn't she? Who was he to intrude?

He turned to leave, but a small sound she made, a sound filled with such anguish, had him turning back around again.

"Hannah." He stood behind her, called her name softly. "Tell me what's wrong."

Her shoulders hunched forward, and she shook her head. "I'm fine," she said between sobs.

Seth had never known how to handle a woman's tears. He'd never been any good at this stuff, never knew what to say or what to do. This time, with Hannah, was no different. He warred with himself over staying or leaving, then swore silently and reached for a paper towel.

"Here." He shoved the makeshift tissue in front of her.

"Thank you." She took the paper towel and wiped at her face. "I'll be all right. I'll start dinner in a—"

"Forget dinner, dammit." He dragged a hand through his hair, then said more gently, "I want to help, Hannah. At least tell me what's wrong."

She was silent for a long moment, then she sighed heavily and handed him the letter sitting on the counter, the one she'd opened in the living room. She kept her back to him while he glanced at it.

"Hannah," Seth read,

I know I told you that this check would be for more, but this is all I can manage for now. I'm still waiting on the fee from the Owen property sale. Should be in any day, sweetheart, so here's a token of my good faith until the real money comes in. Give me a month or two and I'll catch up on the back payments.

Love, Brent.

"I take it that this is your ex-husband," Seth said tightly after glancing at the check.

She nodded.

"Child support?" he asked, and when she nodded again, he felt a muscle jump in his jaw. It was bad enough the bastard wasn't sending the money he was supposed to, he had the nerve to call Hannah "sweetheart" and sign the letter "love."

Sight unseen, Seth would like to punch the guy in the mouth.

"How many months is he behind?"

Hannah sighed, then wrapped her arms tightly around herself. "It doesn't matter, Seth."

"Like hell it doesn't matter," he said sharply. "Of course it matters."

She turned to look at him. "I'll figure something out."

"What happens if you don't?"

She drew in a long, slow breath, then pressed her lips tightly together. "My aunt is half owner of this house. Unless I can pay my share of the rent or buy her out, I'll have to sell."

"And you'd give up living here?" he asked. "Give up your bed-and-breakfast?"

"Sometimes a person doesn't have a choice," she said, the exhaustion in her voice and reddened eyes apparent.

"You have a choice." He leveled his gaze with hers. "You can let me help you."

Her brow furrowed. "How can you help me?"

"I have a few thousand—"

"No." She shook her head emphatically. "Absolutely not."

"Hannah, for crying out loud, you can't just—"

"No, Seth. This is my problem, not yours. I appreciate the offer, and I thank you. But I can't."

"You could pay me back in—"

"*No.*"

Frustrated, he frowned at her. "Anyone ever tell you that you're stubborn?"

"Never."

He glanced up at the ceiling, shook his head. "I've never met another woman like you, Hannah Michaels."

"What?" She laughed dryly. "Stubborn, foolish, plain, dull—"

"Is that how you see yourself?" he asked quietly. "Is that what you think you are, plain and dull?"

She shrugged awkwardly. "Well, for heaven's sake, I'm not exactly Sally Siren."

She believed that, he thought incredulously. She really believed all that nonsense.

He could tell her that she was wrong, very wrong, but knew she wouldn't believe him. And since he'd made that damn promise not to touch her, it was going to be a little difficult to show her.

"Hannah." He put his hands on the counter, one on either side of her, and leaned in close. "That's the biggest bunch of bull I've ever heard."

She stiffened, then her cheeks flamed red. "It is?" she said, her voice small and tight.

"Yeah." He dropped his head closer to hers, breathed in the faint, floral scent of her perfume. "And you know what else?"

"What?" Her voice was barely audible.

"I think you're just about the sexiest woman I've ever seen."

She inched her head back and frowned. "Now I know you're lying."

"I wouldn't lie, Hannah. Not to you." He saw the suspicion in her eyes, but he saw something else, too. Desire. When she licked her lips in a nervous gesture, Seth felt his blood heat up and rush through his veins. "Do you want to know what I was thinking when I watched you get out of your car a few minutes ago?"

"What's for dinner?" she said weakly.

He shook his head, refusing to let her retreat behind humor. "I was wondering who you'd been with last night and today. I was thinking whoever it was, he was one lucky guy."

Her eyes widened with surprise. "I was filling in for

Kristina Bridges at the Trail Drive steak house. She's a hostess there, and she needed her weekend shift covered. Why would you think I'd been with a man?''

''Why wouldn't I think that?'' he asked. ''A woman who looks like you, alone for the weekend. All dressed up.''

''Dressed up?'' She glanced down at the skirt she wore. ''I've had this forever.''

''It's pretty.'' He brought his mouth close to her ear and whispered, ''I was wondering how many buttons I'd have to undo before it would slide down those long, gorgeous legs of yours.''

''Oh.'' She swallowed hard and shuddered. *Probably five or six.*

Smiling, he dropped his gaze to her mouth and murmured, ''And I was wondering what you had on underneath. Practical soft cotton...or smooth silk.''

She did not respond, but she let her head fall back as she gazed up at him. Her eyelids were heavy, her breathing quick and shallow. Seth had started this, but if it was to go any further, it was up to Hannah. He wasn't certain he could take much more himself, though.

''Hannah,'' he said huskily, ''I want you. I want to make love to you.''

Still she said nothing, made no move toward him. Her breasts rose and fell as she looked at him. She had to ask him, dammit. He thought he might die if she didn't, but he wouldn't touch her unless she said the words.

''Seth,'' she said at last, her voice a breathless whisper, ''before you make love to me, do you think you could kiss me first?''

Eight

In her entire life, Hannah had never asked a man to even kiss her, let alone make love to her. And while the thought of asking still seemed awkward to her, the actual asking had not.

She wanted Seth to kiss her, to touch her, to make love with her. How desperately she wanted that, how much she wanted *him*, shocked her.

She slid her hands up his chest, felt the ripple of hard muscle under her palms. His eyes glinted like black fire as he looked down at her.

"Kiss me." She curled her fingers into the soft cotton of his T-shirt and pulled him closer. "Kiss me."

His mouth swooped down and caught hers at the same time his arms came around her. She pressed against him, wanting to be closer still. How wonderful he felt, she thought. The rock-solid feel of his tall, muscular body; the masculine scent of his skin; the taste of mint and chocolate in his mouth. Her head spun with the sensations swirling through her, her heart raced, her blood pounded in her ears.

She wrapped her arms around his strong neck, met the hard, hot thrust of his tongue with her own. He deepened the kiss and she joined him, thrust after hungry thrust. Her skin tightened, her breasts ached with a need she'd never experienced before. How she wanted his hands on her, everywhere, and it amazed her how much she wanted her hands on him, as well.

With a moan, he dragged his mouth from hers. "Hannah, come to my bedroom," he said raggedly. "Come to my bed."

When she nodded he released her, then took her hand and brought it to his mouth. "Say it," he murmured. "Tell me that you want me. That you want this. Be sure."

"I'm sure, Seth." She shivered when his mouth moved over her hand and his teeth lightly nipped each knuckle. Currents of electricity shot up her arm. "I want you. I want you to make love to me."

The distance down the hall was short, but it seemed like the longest journey of Hannah's life. With every step, logic threatened to intrude, while reason whispered warnings. He sensed her uncertainty, kissed her, whispered things no man had ever said to her, things that made her blush, things that thrilled and excited her. He told her what he wanted to do, how beautiful she was, how sexy.

What truly amazed her was that she believed him. She *felt* beautiful, she felt sexy. She wanted him to do all the things to her that he'd said he would; she wanted to do things to him, too. Things she'd never done before.

Light from the swiftly setting sun cast the bedroom in hazy shades of gray. Shadows filled the corners and dusk settled like a warm blanket. Seth closed the door and pulled her into his arms again, kissing her even as he led her across the room.

She held on to him, rose up on tiptoes to fit her body to his when they stopped beside the bed. His hands slid over her shoulders, then down her back to her buttocks. He cupped her in his hands, caressed her as he pulled her intimately against him. The contact sent spears of fire shooting through her blood.

His mouth blazed kisses down her neck and she dropped her head back, allowing him more freedom. She shivered at the hot breath whispering over her cheek, shuddered when his teeth nipped at her earlobe, moaned when his tongue slid over the curve of her ear.

She heard the ragged sound of her breathing mix with Seth's, felt his hands tighten on her rear end and move against her in a time-old rhythm of mating. He was hard, as ready for her as she was for him, but he did not seem to be in a hurry, a fact which excited her as much as frustrated her.

This was what all the commotion about sex was about, she thought dimly. She'd heard all the whispered giggling among the women she knew, listened to Lori's and Phoebe's blatant confessions of ecstasy in the bedroom. But she'd never really believed it, never felt it before. Sex had been all right, but nothing that made her feel as if she'd been turned inside out, as if every single cell in her body was raw and exposed, vibrating with need.

While his mouth, his magical, amazing mouth, moved down her neck, she slid her hands up his strong arms. He'd wakened her senses to a level she'd never experienced before. Under her fingertips, she felt the solid, firm texture of his skin, the light sprinkling of hair on his forearms, the sinew of muscle. Her hands moved over his broad shoulders then continued up his neck. When he lifted his face to gaze down at her, she cupped his face in her hands, felt the light stubble of beard against her palm, the sensation like tiny bolts of lightning shooting from her fingertips to her toes.

"Seth," she whispered. "What are you doing to me?"

"If you don't know," he said, his voice tight with passion, his dark eyes narrowed and fierce, "I must not be doing it right."

"Oh, you're doing it right." She wrapped her arms around his neck, then brought his mouth to hers. "You're definitely doing it more than right."

He kissed her hard and deep, moved his hands over her hips and molded her curves in his palms. His fingers found the waistband of her skirt, flicked the top button from its hole, then another as he moved downward. Her skirt floated around her legs, then swirled to the floor, pooling around her feet.

"Four," he murmured softly.

"Four?"

"It took four buttons to slip this skirt off you." His hands moved over her bottom again. "You're wearing silk."

"Mystery solved," she said, then shivered when he moved his large, callused hands down the sides of her thighs, then the fronts, his fingertips only inches from the V of her legs. "Now it's my turn."

She reached for the hem of his T-shirt and pulled upward. He helped her by tugging the garment off and tossing it aside. She'd seen his chest before, the first day she'd met him, but it was different now. So very different. *She* was different.

Boldly, she laid her palms flat on his chest and pressed her lips to his warm skin, felt the tickle of coarse hair against her nose and cheek. When she brazenly kissed his flat nipple, then licked it with her tongue, he sucked in a breath and raked his hands up her back and into her hair. Gently he tugged her head back while he kissed her again and again, until she felt dizzy and her knees went weak.

The mattress dipped underneath them when they sank to the edge of the bed together. The shadows surrounding them had grown, but there was still enough light to see. She inched back and let her eyes feast on him. His height and powerful body had intimidated her a little at first, but now they aroused her. She wanted to feel him on top of her, underneath her, inside her.

Her knuckles grazed the smooth, warm skin on his belly when she reached for the snap on his jeans and pulled it free. She felt his dark, fierce gaze on her as she slid his zipper slowly down.

"Wait." His hand covered hers.

Confused, she watched as he moved away, then rifled through his black travel bag. After a moment, he straightened, then set the matchbook-sized package on the nightstand.

Protection. Hannah closed her eyes, then laid her forehead on his chest when he sat back down beside her. "Thank you," she whispered. "I—I wasn't thinking."

"Good." He cupped her face in his hands and brought his lips whisper-close to hers. "I don't want you thinking."

As he laid her back on the bed and covered her mouth

with his, he got his wish. She couldn't think at all, could barely breathe. She felt the hunger in his kiss, tasted the passion, but it wasn't enough. She needed more.

He obliged her. His mouth left hers, moved down her neck while his hands slid up her bare thighs and belly. He caught the hem of her tank top in his hands and inch by agonizing inch he slipped the garment up and then over her head.

He gazed down at her, his eyes dark with primal heat. Slowly he traced the lace edge of her bra with his fingertip, making her shiver with anticipation. "You're so beautiful," he murmured and lowered his head.

She gasped at the first touch of his mouth on her skin. His lips followed the same path his fingertip had taken while his hands slid up her belly to mold her breasts in his palms. Hannah squirmed under his touch, felt her heart slam against her ribs. *Hurry,* she wanted to say, but she seemed incapable of speech. Moaning, she raked her fingernails over his shoulders, then slid her hand up into his long, thick hair.

In one smooth motion he flicked open the front clasp of her bra, then pushed satin and lace aside. She arched upward when he took the sensitive tip of her breast into his mouth. He stroked her with his hot, wet tongue and she dug her fingers into his scalp. While his hands kneaded and caressed, he sucked gently on her hardened nipple, sending arrows of white-hot pleasure directly to that most sensitive place at the juncture of her thighs. She writhed under him as he rose then dropped down again and gave equal attention to her other breast.

This was *too* wonderful, she thought, and wondered if a person truly could die from pleasure this intense. And when he moved one hand down her belly, slipped his hand under her panties, then slid into the moist heat of her body, she was certain a person *could* die. He set the rhythm and gasping, she moved with him, felt the fire burning inside her as he stroked her.

"Seth, please," she managed. "Please."

He moved away, tugged his jeans and briefs down, then kicked them off. A moment later he stood at the edge of the bed, staring down at her. He leaned forward, slid her panties off, then moved between her legs. He lowered himself, then locked his gaze with hers as he entered her.

His hands slipped under her hips, and she rose to meet him as he filled her. Again and again he moved inside her, until she was gasping his name. She felt as if she were on fire. A fire that grew hotter and hotter, the flames burning out of control.

Her world shattered at the same time as her body. She cried out in amazement and shock as the shimmering waves of color and light rolled through her and crashed onto an unseen shore.

Exhilarated, she held on to Seth's strong shoulders, then brought him rolling and shuddering with her.

He held her close to him, her back pressing against his chest and her bottom nestled intimately against his groin. She'd fallen asleep several minutes after they'd made love, and he listened to the rhythmic, soft sound of her breathing, felt the steady beat of her pulse under his hands. He pressed a light kiss to her bare shoulder, then slipped off the bed and gently covered her with the down comforter. She sighed and stirred, but she didn't wake.

Moonlight lit the room in tones that resembled a black-and-white photograph. Seth snagged his jeans lying on the floor and tugged them on, then his T-shirt.

He stood beside the bed and gazed down at Hannah. Her hands were curled up under her chin, her blond curls tumbled around her face and across the pillow. A soft smile curved her kiss-swollen lips.

He felt the desire rise again, felt his blood heat up, but he'd let her sleep. Lord knew the woman needed it.

And, if he were to be honest with himself, he wasn't so certain he was ready to touch her so soon again. He wanted her, no doubt about that. If anything, now that they had made love, he wanted her more than he had before.

He'd made love to other women, had always enjoyed sex, but he'd never met a woman before who'd made him forget where he was or who he was. With Hannah, he felt...out of balance. It disturbed him that he wasn't completely in control. He didn't like it.

He slipped quietly out of the room and headed for the kitchen. He knew she'd be hungry when she woke up, and his own stomach was letting him know it was past time to eat. He was no Emeril, but he supposed he could throw something together.

He found carrots in the refrigerator, which he cut up and dumped in a pan with some water, then washed some big potatoes from the pantry and popped them in the microwave and turned it on. He discovered a bottle of cabernet in a top cupboard and opened it, then remembered the steaks she'd brought home from the restaurant. They were still sitting wrapped on the counter, next to the letter from her ex.

With a frown, Seth picked up the letter and looked at it again. Michaels Realty, the letterhead read. Brent Michaels, owner and developer. Four Oaks, Texas.

Four Oaks was only a couple of hours from here, Seth knew. So why didn't this jerk come see his kids? Why wasn't he the one who took them to camp? And the biggest question of all, why the hell wasn't he still here, with his family?

Seth thought about Maddie and Missy. They were both beautiful, terrific little girls. How could a man walk away from his own kids? Five minutes alone with Brent Michaels, that's all he wanted, Seth thought as he stuffed the letter back into the envelope. Five minutes just to "talk" with the guy.

Hannah might not want his help financially, but there were other ways he could help, Seth knew. And if he played his cards right, she'd never even have to know.

"Hey."

He turned at the sound of Hannah's voice. She stood in the doorway, her hands locked behind her back as she watched him. She'd pulled her skirt and tank top back on, but he could see she wasn't wearing a bra. Heat shot straight to his groin, and though his first impulse was to take her back to bed, he quickly tamped it down. He *could* control himself, dammit, he told himself. He could, and he would.

"Hey, yourself."

He took a wineglass out of the cupboard and filled it. When he moved toward her, he could see the blush on her cheeks and the hesitation in her eyes. He wouldn't give her time to think, he decided, and pulled her against him. He brought his mouth to hers and kissed her long and hard and deep.

When he stepped back, she gripped the doorjamb with her hand to steady herself.

"You're supposed to be sleeping," he said and handed her the glass of wine.

Her lips, still moist from his kiss, touched the rim of the glass. She took a sip of wine, then handed it back to him. "More than ten minutes and I wouldn't sleep tonight."

"I've got news for you, darlin'." One corner of his mouth curved up as he pulled her to him again. "You *aren't* sleeping tonight."

He brushed his lips across hers, pressed the wineglass back into her shaky hand and moved away. If he kissed her the way he wanted to, they'd be back in the bedroom in two seconds flat.

When he turned the broiler on, she started toward him. "Here, I can—"

"You." He turned and pointed a finger at her. "Sit. I'm making dinner for you."

"Well, at least let me—"

"Hannah. Sit."

She pressed her lips into a thin line, then sat stiffly in the chair. Twice he saw her start to rise, but he warned her back both times.

He had the carrots cooking and steaks broiling in a matter of minutes, then took plates out of the cupboard and utensils out of the drawer. He drained the carrots, swore when he lost half of them in the sink, then pulled the potatoes out of the microwave and poked at them with a fork. He had no idea how anything would taste, but at least it didn't look half bad, he thought.

Needing something to do with her hands, Hannah continued to sip the wine Seth had given her. She rarely drank, but if ever it seemed like an appropriate time to imbibe, it was now. She was still reeling from making love with Seth, and though it was making her crazy to sit here and not help with dinner, she wasn't certain her legs would hold her up at the moment.

So she watched him move awkwardly around the kitchen, biting her lip to keep from making suggestions or offering her help. She winced when he burned himself taking the steaks out of the oven, but still he refused her help, slid her a look of utter exasperation when she suggested he run his hand under cold water.

When he filled a plate and set it in front of her, all she could do was stare at the food. A man making dinner and fussing over her was a completely new experience for her. It felt odd, but it felt wonderful at the same time.

But Seth's making dinner for her wasn't her only new experience, she thought. Heat shimmered through her body as she remembered his lovemaking. He'd been tender, but he'd been strong and forceful, too. His touch, his scent, his taste, all of him still lingered on her skin.

Her throat felt thick and moisture burned her eyes. She took a sip of wine and glanced away, blinked furiously as she told herself she was being silly and childish and overly emotional. She was a grown woman, for heaven's sake.

"Hannah, what's wrong?" A frown on his face, Seth knelt beside her and took the wineglass from her hands. "We can order pizza if it's that bad," he said. "Or how 'bout eggs? I know how to cook eggs. If you like scrambled, anyway."

She shook her head. "It's not the food, Seth. It's me."

"What's you?"

Smiling, she reached out and touched his cheek with her hand, felt that same jolt of electricity she felt every time she touched him. "You...I..." She hesitated. "When we made love...I, well, that was the first time I ever..."

She couldn't say it. It was too embarrassing. She

pulled her hand from his cheek and looked away, couldn't bear it if he teased or laughed at her.

"Hannah." He took hold of her arms and pulled her from the chair, then sat down and tugged her onto his lap. "You're twenty-six years old, you've been married and have children and you're saying that you never—"

"No." She couldn't bear to hear him say it, either. "I haven't."

He took her chin in his hand and turned her face to his. "Look at me."

Relief poured through her when she lifted her gaze to his. She saw amazement in his eyes, but there was no laughter, no ridicule, and she let herself relax against him.

"What the hell kind of idiot were you married to, anyway?" he asked her. "And *why* did you marry him?"

His question caught her off guard, but it was easier to go in that direction than to discuss herself. She shrugged, let herself enjoy the pleasure and intimacy of sliding her hand over Seth's broad chest.

"My mom was ill when I was in high school," she said quietly. "With my dad already gone, I needed to take care of her, so I didn't have the experiences of dating or parties or activities that the other kids had."

"So you and your ex weren't high-school sweethearts?"

She smiled at that. "No. I met Brent one year after I graduated high school and three months after my mom died. He'd just moved here from Dallas to set up a housing development deal for the company he worked for at the time. He was the ultimate salesman, charming, handsome, attentive and persistent. I fell in love with that man. I think the only reason he married me was because he was bored living in Ridgewater. That, and because I wouldn't sleep with him while we were dating. He lost out on both counts.''

Seth's arms tightened around her. "Hannah, for God's sake, stop saying that. You're sexy and beautiful and one hell of a mother. If he couldn't see that, then the guy is as blind as he is stupid.''

"Thank you.'' She laid her head on his shoulder and traced the outline of his collarbone with her fingertip. "For a long time, I blamed myself. I wasn't pretty enough or sophisticated enough or sexy enough. When he starting traveling more and working late hours, I knew he was seeing another woman. It hurt terribly, but the bottom line was, between taking care of a house and twins and working part-time, I just didn't care. Sex had never been that interesting to me, and if anything, it became a relief he didn't want to make love to me. It was easier to look the other way. When he finally did leave, I was beyond caring. I had the girls and that was all that really mattered to me. It's all that really matters now.''

She lifted her head and grinned at him. "Though now that you've enlightened me to certain aspects of life I've been missing, I may have to make some adjustments. Maybe find a little time to start dating more.''

He frowned darkly at her. "Don't get carried away, Hannah. Too much of a good thing can be dangerous.''

"Not *too* much,'' she teased. "A Friday-night date here and—''

She gasped when he suddenly snatched her to him and covered her mouth with his. The kiss was rough, as intense as it was hungry. Every bone in her body seemed to soften, and she melted against him. Desire shot through her like an arrow and once again she wanted him.

"Make love to me, Seth," she said raggedly when his mouth finally left hers. "Please."

"Darlin', that you can count on," he said, his voice tight with passion, but when she started to lean into him, he held her back. "But first you're going to eat. You're going to need all your strength tonight."

"Oh?" She smiled coyly, looked up at him as she spread her hands on his chest. "And why is that?"

He leaned down and whispered in her ear what he wanted to do to her later. She shuddered at the sensuous words, then sat down at the table and hoped that they could both eat fast.

Sunday morning came much too quickly. Hannah slept on her stomach, curled peacefully under the sheets with her face half-buried in a fluffy pillow. Lying on his side, elbow bent and his head resting in the palm of his hand, Seth watched the gentle rise and fall of her shoulders. He resisted the urge to press his lips to her bare skin, resisted the urge to slip his hand under the sheets and smooth his palm down her back and over the rounded curve of her bottom. Resisted the urge to wake her and do much, much more.

For the moment, though, he was content to simply watch her sleep.

Besides, after the night they'd spent together, he knew she needed her rest. He also knew that Maddie and Missy wouldn't be coming home until much later on in the evening, which meant that he and Hannah had all day together, to do whatever they pleased. And a nice big house to do it in, he thought with a smile.

She stirred then, rustling the sheets as she rolled to

her back. Her eyelashes fluttered open and for a moment, she seemed disoriented. Then her eyes opened wide, and she glanced at him.

"Mornin'," he said.

"So it wasn't a dream."

Her sleepy voice slid over his skin, made his pulse quicken and his blood warm. He grinned at her, lowered his mouth to hers and kissed her. She smiled against his lips as she stretched, then wrapped her arms around his neck and pulled him closer.

The kiss deepened; grew urgent and greedy. He snatched the sheet from her and she wrapped her long, sleek legs around his waist, tempting him, teasing him. He slid inside her on a moan, heard the roar of his heartbeat in his head. He lost himself in the velvet glove of her body, the satin texture and woman scent of her skin, the soft little moans that rose from deep in her throat. Everything about her aroused him, made him ache with a need he'd never experienced before.

"Hannah," he said raggedly. "Open your eyes."

She seemed lost somewhere, drifting on a sea of passion, her back arched, her face flushed and eyes closed.

"Open your eyes," he repeated. "Look at me."

Her lids opened slowly; she looked at him with desire-glazed eyes. He rose over her, slid his hands up her flat, smooth belly, then cupped her breasts in his palms. When he rubbed her hard nipples with his thumbs, her blue eyes darkened to cobalt. She sucked in a breath, bit her bottom lip and moaned as he lowered his head to one pebbled tip and closed his mouth over her.

"Seth," she gasped, dragging her hands through his hair. "Now, please, now."

Her soft plea snapped what little control he'd been clinging to. He moved deep inside her, felt her body convulse and shudder. And then he shuddered, too, held her tight as they tumbled together over the edge.

It was several minutes before he rolled off her, then gathered her close again. She nestled her cheek against his chest, snuggled against him in the crook of his arm with a contented sigh.

"I may never move again," she murmured.

He smiled, slid his hand over to cup her breast. "Wanna bet?"

She shook her head. "I'd lose that one."

He kissed her temple, then moved downward to nibble at her ear. "I say we stay naked and in bed all day."

"What about food?" She traced circles on his chest with her fingertip. "One of us has to get out of bed to cook."

"We can order pizza and have them leave it on the front porch."

"Pizza for breakfast?"

"A bachelor's main staple. That and canned chili."

She was silent for a long moment, her fingertip still moving restlessly over his chest now. Then she said, "How come you aren't married?"

It was a simple question, and she wondered why he took so long to answer. She'd bared everything to him, her body, her soul, and God help her, her heart. It hurt to think that revealing even a little part of himself, of who he was and why, would be difficult. She started to rise when he tightened his hold on her and held her in place.

"I'm a cop," he said evenly. "Not a nine-to-five, five-days-a-week cop, that's hard enough on a marriage, but an undercover cop. I'm gone for days, sometimes weeks, at a time and I can't tell anyone where I am. Sometimes it's dangerous, though mostly it's just sitting around in a sleazy bar or hanging around the streets, hoping to gain the trust of someone who's not what you'd consider an upstanding citizen. I've tried relationships, even lived with a woman once. It didn't work out.''

The brief stab of jealousy made Hannah pause. She certainly had no right to feel resentment toward any woman Seth had been with. Undoubtedly he'd been with several.

But the women he'd been with was the last thing she wanted to talk about at the moment. Sliding her hand up his muscled arm to his cheek, she traced his bristled jaw with her fingertips.

''What about your family? Don't your parents worry about you?''

''My dad was killed when I was a teenager,'' Seth said quietly. ''He worked vice and was shot in the line of duty.''

''And now you're a cop?'' Hannah shook her head. ''I can only imagine how much your mother worries about you.''

''She would if she knew. She thinks I work traffic. She retired a couple of years ago and moved to Florida, so I don't talk to her very often.''

''And your sister and brother?'' she asked cautiously. ''You said you don't know where they are?''

His jaw tightened under her fingertips and she felt his body stiffen. Obviously she'd asked the wrong question.

''I'm sorry.'' She sat, pulled the sheets up to cover herself and slid to the edge of the bed. ''I'm prying. I'll just go get some break—''

''Hannah.'' His hand circled her arm and tugged her gently back. ''Come here.''

''Really, Seth, I didn't mean to—''

"Hannah, just be quiet, will you?" He sat up in the bed and pulled her against him. After a long moment, he sighed, then said, "I'm adopted. My real parents were killed when I was seven."

"Oh, Seth." She laid her head on his chest. "I'm so sorry."

He stroked her hair away from her face. "I lived on a small ranch just outside Wolf River with my parents, my older brother Rand and my baby sister Elizabeth."

He paused, but she said nothing, just waited for him to continue.

"I don't remember the night it happened, only what I was told later by my adopted parents, that my family was driving back from town one night, in a storm." His voice had a distant quality to it. "A lightning bolt struck the road directly in front of us and the car swerved over the edge of a mountain cliff, then rolled several times into a ravine."

Hannah closed her eyes, felt the rush of pain and despair wash through her. She knew the ache of losing loved ones, but he'd been so young, a seven-year-old child suddenly without a mother or a father.

"I had a concussion and a broken collarbone, but all in all, I was fine. Everything that happened over the next couple of days is hazy. All I knew was that suddenly I had a new home, a new family and a new name, all in the blink of an eye."

She sat, stared at him in confusion. "You were separated from your sister and brother?"

"I was told they'd died in the accident along with my parents. For the past twenty-three years I've believed that." He dragged a hand through his hair. "Then two weeks ago I received a letter from a lawyer in Wolf River telling me that Rand and Lizzie didn't die. They were adopted out the same as I was."

"Who would do such a despicable thing?" Her fist tightened on the sheets. Such a horrible thing was beyond her comprehension. "And *why* would they?"

Seth shook his head. "That's what I was on my way to find out last week. The lawyer who contacted me told me he'd explain everything when I got to Wolf River."

"Oh, Seth." Hannah sighed and dropped her head into her hand. "You'd be there now if you hadn't saved Maddie."

"Hannah." He lifted her chin with his finger. "Look at me."

When she met his gaze, he said, "I wouldn't change one thing that's happened to me since I came here. Not one thing, you got that?"

"Even the newspaper article?"

He frowned. "Okay, maybe that. But that's it."

"Really?"

"Really."

Smiling, she leaned forward and pressed her lips to his, lingered there for a moment, then drew back with a thoughtful look in her eyes. "What was your last name?" she asked. "Before the Grangers adopted you?"

"Blackhawk." He glanced away, stared blindly across the room. "It was a long time ago, but still I never forgot them. My parents, Rand and Lizzie. I loved the Grangers and they were good parents to me, but there always seemed to be something missing. Something that wasn't quite right."

"Maybe you knew," Hannah said. "Maybe at some

instinctual level, you knew your sister and brother were alive.''

He shrugged. ''Maybe. I'll see what this lawyer has to say when I get to Wolf River. In the meantime—'' he grinned and pulled her into his arms ''—I've got a woman named Sally on my mind.''

''Oh, is that so?'' She rolled away and slid out of bed, then snatched up his white T-shirt from the floor. ''Sally who?''

''Sally Siren.''

She grinned at him and pulled his T-shirt on, ducked away when he made a grab for her. ''Well, I've got George on my mind.''

''Yeah?'' He tossed the sheets aside, a wicked look in his eyes as he reached for his jeans. ''George who?

''You know, *George*.'' She backed toward the door, watched as he yanked on his jeans and started for her. ''The cartoon watch-out-for-that-tree George.''

He lifted a brow, then grinned and beat on his chest as he hunched over and came at her. When he grabbed for her, she laughed, then spun and ran down the hallway with him in hot pursuit. He caught her before she made the foot of the stairs and circled her waist with his arms. She screamed when he tickled her and squirmed to get away, but he held her tight and tormented her.

She was still laughing when his mouth swooped down and caught hers in a hungry kiss. She kissed him back, felt her knees turn to warm taffy and the floor under her feet shift and turn. Wrapping her arms around him, she rose on her tiptoes and pulled him closer, was about to suggest they go back into the bedroom when she heard a small, metallic sound from the front door.

She yanked her mouth from Seth's and turned as the front door opened.

Oh dear God.

Eyes wide, mouth open, Hannah froze and stared into the shocked face of her aunt.

Nine

Alone in the kitchen, a mug of black coffee in his hand, Seth stood at the open window and watched Mrs. Peterson trim her rose bushes while Beau sunned himself on the front lawn, his large jaws busy with a rawhide bone the size of a baseball bat. The steady *clip, clip, clip* of pruning shears mixed with the hum of an unseen lawn mower, and the scent of freshly mowed grass filled the warm air.

It might have been the perfect Sunday morning, if not for the sound of Aunt Martha's shrill, stern voice coming from the living room.

Seth's hand tightened around the mug of coffee that had long since turned cold. Listening to the woman severely chastise her niece had made it impossible for him to swallow. Even harder was listening to Hannah's submissive replies to her aunt's verbal lashing.

When Aunt Martha had barged through the front door

thirty minutes ago, the expression of horror on the woman's face had nearly been laughable. But Hannah had obviously found nothing humorous about the compromising situation her aunt had walked in on. He'd felt Hannah tremble in his arms, had heard her sharp intake of breath. Clearly, Hannah had not been expecting the woman.

And clearly, Aunt Martha had not been expecting to find her niece standing at the foot of the stairs with a strange man, both of them half-naked.

The woman's face had gone from bone-white to scarlet in the blink of an eye, a sharp contrast to the chic, slim-fitting chocolate-colored sheath dress she wore. She was an attractive woman, probably in her sixties. Her silver hair was fashionably short, her makeup fastidious, her long nails the same bronze tone as her lips. With wide eyes, she'd stared at them in disbelief, her hand still frozen on the door. On that same hand, she wore a diamond that probably cost more money than he'd even made last year.

Hannah had been the first one to move. She'd tugged frantically at the hem of the T-shirt she wore—*his* T-shirt—babbled about what a surprise it was to see her aunt, made an attempt at introductions, then dashed up the stairs. Her lips pressed into a tight line, Aunt Martha turned her narrowed, piercing gaze back to him, looked him up and down, then closed the door behind her and marched into the living room without so much as a word.

It didn't take a genius to figure out neither woman wanted him around at that moment. It had taken tremendous effort, but he'd resisted the temptation to go after Hannah when she'd run up the stairs. Instead, he'd gone back to his room and slipped on a T-shirt and tennis shoes, then headed for the kitchen and the coffeemaker.

Some people said that music soothed the savage beast. For him, it was strong black coffee.

And after catching bits and pieces of what Aunt Martha was saying to Hannah—*irresponsible, promiscuous* and *improper* were a few of the words spewing from the woman's mouth—*savage* was a good word to describe what he was feeling. The only problem was, the coffee wasn't working. Minute by minute, as he listened to Hannah's aunt harangue her, his blood burned hotter and his anger turned darker.

"...your inexcusable behavior..." Seth heard Aunt Martha say from the other room. His hand tightened on the mug he held; a muscle jumped in his jaw. He needed to get out of the house before he said or did something stupid. As much as he'd like to tell the old biddy off, he knew he wouldn't be doing Hannah any favors if he interfered.

He turned, started for the door to the hallway and laundry area, intending to slip out the back door. But even in the hallway, the sound of Aunt Martha's voice burned the air.

"I've been exceedingly patient with you," the woman said stiffly. "A three-months' extension has been more than generous on my part, Hannah. If you can't be prompt with a simple payment on your share of the rent, then how do you expect ever to run a successful business? You'll fail before you've even seen your first customer."

Seth ground his teeth, told himself to keep walking. *None of your business,* he told himself. Control had always been more than important to Seth, it had been essential. In his job, control, or the lack of it, could mean the difference between life and death. He'd learned to think before he spoke, to calculate the consequences before he made a move.

Yet he stayed at the base of the stairs and listened. Why didn't Hannah respond? he wondered. Why didn't she tell her aunt to butt out?

"What would your mother think, God rest her soul?" Martha continued. "Her own daughter having a shameful tryst with a man she's just met. It's disgraceful, Hannah Louise."

Anger slashed through Seth, hot and sharp. *Answer her, dammit,* he thought. *Tell her to go to hell.*

But she didn't. Seth curled his hands into fists and turned back toward the hallway. He couldn't stay here and listen to this. He needed to get out now.

"What kind of woman does that make you?" Martha said shrilly. "What kind of mother?"

Like an arctic blast, Martha's pious, insulting comment froze Seth where he stood.

That did it.

He turned slowly, made his way to the living room. Wearing a pair of black dress slacks and a soft pink silk blouse, Hannah sat on the sofa, her back straight as a board. She stared down at the hands she'd linked tightly in her lap. Her face was pale, her lips pressed firmly together. Aunt Martha stood in front of the brick fireplace, her arms folded, her nose lifted in the air as if there were a bad smell in the room.

"Were you thinking about your children?" Aunt Martha said coolly. "Were you thinking about how this might—"

"Stop." Seth moved into the room, startling both women. "You just stop right there."

"Seth." Panic lit Hannah's face as she rose from the sofa. "It's all right."

"It's not all right, dammit." He stared at the elder woman and tried to understand how Hannah could be related to such a patronizing witch. The scent of her expensive perfume filled the room, made him want to throw every window open and pray for a cleansing breeze. "I won't—can't—just stand by and let you talk to her like that."

"This is none of your concern." Aunt Martha narrowed her disapproving eyes at him. "I'll ask you to leave immediately."

"You can ask all you want." He moved into the room. "And I'm making it my concern."

"Seth, please." Hannah moved between him and her aunt. "This isn't helping."

"It's helping me." He kept his gaze on Martha, felt the icy chill of her gaze. "Have you any idea how hard this woman works to take care of this house and her daughters? Did you know she gets up every morning at four-thirty just to bake muffins to bring in a few extra dollars? That she works two jobs outside the house, plus any side jobs she's offered?"

Hannah touched his shoulder, whispered his name as she exhaled. He heard her desperation, felt it in her touch, but still couldn't stop himself. "Did you know she's been remodeling this place practically by herself, that her good for nothing ex-husband hasn't given her more than a few dollars in months?"

Clearly she hadn't known that, Seth decided. Aunt Martha's surprised gaze darted to Hannah and her hand went to her throat.

"Hannah, why didn't you—"

The woman stopped, then lifted her chin and said

crisply, "She doesn't have to live like this. I've offered my niece a lovely home to live in and private schools for her girls. Boston is rich in culture and civility. What does Ridgewater have, other than an absurd, oversized mass of fruit and nuts?"

"It's got heart, for one thing," Seth said tightly. "Something you seem to have misplaced."

Martha's eyes widened at the verbal barb, then she squared her shoulders and lifted her chin. "I entertain a great deal, could connect Hannah to all the right people. People who could help her find a suitable position."

"She's got a suitable position." Seth barely noticed Hannah's hand tightening on his arm. "Right here. In this house, in this town. A single mother on her own, and the best damn mother those girls could hope to have. She's also twenty-six years old, and shouldn't have to explain or justify whatever happens in the privacy of her own house to anyone. Especially to someone who doesn't have the courtesy to call, or even knock, before she walks in unannounced and uninvited."

"Please," Hannah pleaded. "Seth, let me handle this. Please."

"I refuse to stand here and listen to any more of this." Aunt Martha shot an icy gaze at Hannah. "Obviously your taste in men has not improved, my dear. I'll be on the next flight out."

"Aunt Martha, no. Don't go." Hannah touched her aunt's arm, but the woman merely shrugged her off.

"When you come to your senses, Hannah Louise, call me and maybe we can talk." Martha picked up her small, brown-leather shoulder bag and headed for the front door. "Either way, you've proven to me that you're making all the wrong choices. I'm putting this house up for sale next month.''

Hannah's face paled. "No. Please. Just give me time and I'll make up the back payments. I just need a little more time.''

"I've been more than patient with you. I realize it's difficult for you to face another failure in your life, but once you and the girls come to Boston, you'll thank me.''

The woman shot one long, withering look at Seth, then marched out the front door. Hannah started to follow, then stopped and hugged her arms close to her. "What have you done, Seth?'' she murmured. "Oh, God, what have you done?''

"I couldn't let her talk to you that way,'' he said gently and came up behind her. "You didn't deserve that, any of those things she said.''

Hannah turned to face him, anger lighting her blue eyes. "She always talks like that when she's upset. If I let her rant for a while, she calms down. I could have bought a little more time. Now I don't know.''

"Dammit, Hannah.'' He spun away from her, dragged a hand through his hair. "She's a bully and a snob.''

"She's also half owner of this house. She can sell if she wants to, without my permission.''

"Banks give loans to small businesses,'' he insisted. "You have friends here who would help. *I* would help.''

"No.'' She shook her head emphatically. "Banks don't loan money to single mothers with no collateral. I refuse to borrow money from friends, and I most certainly will *not* borrow money from you.''

He winced inwardly at her words, felt a muscle jump

in his jaw. "You don't need her, Hannah. You don't
need that kind of abuse."

"You don't know me well enough to know what I
need," she said tightly. "In a few days you'll be back
on the road and I'll still be here, trying to get from one
day to the next. You had no right to interfere."

"For God's sake, Hannah, will you just—"

"I don't want to talk about this anymore." She
turned away, reached for her purse on the end table and
pulled out her car keys. "Why don't you drive into
town and have a look around? There's a diner that
serves four-egg omelettes and the best hash you'll ever
eat, or there's a tavern with a pool table and darts. The
girls won't be home until seven and I could use the
time to work around here."

He narrowed his eyes, felt the cold settle in his gut.
"If you want me to leave, just say so."

"I thought that's what I just did."

He reached for the keys, covered her hand with his.
"I mean, if you want me to pack up and go, tell me."

She went stiff for a moment, then lifted her gaze to
his. She looked tired, he thought. Weary.

"If I wanted you to 'pack up and go,'" she said
quietly, "I'd tell you. I just need a little time alone,
that's all."

He didn't want to leave her alone, dammit. Not like
this. And he sure as hell didn't like getting kicked out,
either.

Dammit, anyway.

He started to reach for her when the phone rang. She
moved to the side table and answered it, then turned
back to him.

"It's for you." She handed the receiver to him. "A
Lieutenant Jarris."

Jarris. *Dammit.*

"Yeah?" Seth met Hannah's flat, steady gaze as he spoke into the phone, then said after a moment, "Two weeks is the best I can do."

While Jarris barked at him from the other end of the line, Seth watched Hannah turn stiffly and move up the stairs.

Dammit, dammit.

"I'll get there when I get there," Seth said tightly, then slammed down the phone. He scrubbed a hand over his face, then stared at the empty stairs.

This definitely had not been one of his better days.

Hannah sat at her kitchen table and ran through the figures in front of her one more time, at least the tenth time in the past hour. It didn't seem to matter how she rearranged the numbers, the outcome still remained the same: she simply couldn't come up with enough money to pacify her aunt or satisfy the bills she was already late on.

Dropping her elbows on the table, she rested her forehead in the palms of her hands. The base of her skull throbbed, and her eyes had long since blurred from staring at the columns of numbers. Exhaustion seeped into her bones, had her laying her head down on her arms. It wasn't exhaustion of a physical nature, even though she'd had little sleep last night, but rather an emotional and mental exhaustion.

The first two hours after Seth had left the house, she'd thrown herself into sanding the final cracks in the upstairs bedroom. She'd taken a shower after that, let the hot water beat down on her stiff neck and shoulders while she rehashed the morning's events over and over in her mind.

Aunt Martha would never forgive her, Hannah was certain. No one ever spoke to the wealthy and influential Martha Richman that way. At least, Hannah had never *heard* anyone speak to her the way Seth had. Her aunt had been visibly shocked.

In spite of herself, in spite of the situation, Hannah smiled.

And though she was certain her aunt would never forgive her, Hannah was just as certain her aunt would come back around. Aunt Martha would speak to her again—sometime—but Hannah knew that she would have to hear about this incident for a long time to come. Like forever. And the chances of her aunt changing her mind about the rent were somewhere between slim and none. Just about the same odds for Hannah coming up with enough money not only for her bills, but to keep her house, as well.

And as far as the bed-and-breakfast went, she couldn't even think about that now. If she didn't figure out a solution to her financial situation, opening up the Wild Rose would become a moot point.

She'd think of something. She *would*. She hadn't come this far to lose everything now.

She glanced at the clock on her stove. It was nearly four o'clock and she needed to start dinner soon. She had no way of knowing when Seth would return, but she wanted to have a meal prepared in case he came home hungry.

Home. Strange how easy it had become to use that word when she thought of him. This wasn't his home, of course. She understood he was just "passing through," as the expression went, understood that the phone call today from his boss was probably another assignment, that he'd be going to Wolf River, then back to New Mexico.

She also understood that what had happened between them was physical. An extremely pleasurable, mutual night of passion between a man and a woman. Most men and women would accept that situation, move on with their lives when the time came to go their own way.

She wished to God she was most people, wished that her heart could understand what her brain did, that Seth would be leaving soon, that she would probably never see him again. Wished to God that it didn't matter nearly as much as it did.

And if wishes were nickels, her mother used to say, we'd all be rich.

With a heavy sigh, Hannah laid her head in the crook of her elbow and listened to the sounds of the neighborhood drift in through her open window: the Clark children splashing in their pool two doors down, Charlie Hanson's electric hedge trimmers, the hum of Mrs. Peterson's air conditioner. All familiar, all comforting. This was her home, where her grandparents and parents had lived, where she wanted to raise Maddie and Missy.

Her *home,* dammit. Not some glossy, marble-floored showpiece in Boston. *This* house, *this* town, was where she belonged, where her girls belonged. She might go down, she thought, but she sure as hell wouldn't go down without a fight.

She'd work five jobs if she had to. Ten jobs. Whatever it took.

But she just needed a minute to rest. Needed to regroup and gather her strength. Closing her eyes, she let herself drift off. One minute, she told herself, maybe two…

He found her like that thirty minutes later. Bent over the table, her cheek resting on her arms. The sight of her sitting there, sleeping peacefully, made something shift in his chest. His hand tightened around the bouquet of pink carnations he held behind his back, a peace offering, he'd hoped, when he'd picked them up at the local market.

He'd let her sleep, he decided, but hadn't turned before she stirred, furrowing her brow as her eyes fluttered open. With her head still on her arms, she muttered, "What is that heavenly smell?"

"Pizza." He moved into the room, placed the cardboard box on the table and sat across from her. Another peace offering. "I hope you like pepperoni."

"You didn't have to do that." Lifting her head, she yawned, then stretched her arms. "I was going to make dinner."

"Well, if you don't want it—" he started to rise "—I'll just toss it in the trash."

She reached out a hand and grabbed his arm. "Put that back or you die."

Grinning, he sat back down, watched pleasure light her eyes as she lifted the lid of the box. She closed her eyes and breathed in the spicy scent of herbs and tomato. She was reaching for a piece when he pulled the flowers from behind his back.

She went still, stared at the bouquet, then glanced up at him. "Seth, you didn't have to—"

"Stop saying I didn't have to. You're right, I *didn't* have to. I wanted to."

This was new territory for him, apologizing, and he didn't like it. With a frown, he thrust the flowers at her. "Look, I'm sorry I stuck my nose where it didn't belong earlier. You were right. It was none of my business.''

''Thank you.'' Her eyes softened as she took the flowers, then stuck her nose amongst the pretty pink blossoms and breathed in. ''They're beautiful.''

''Tell me what I can do to make things right between you and your aunt.'' He'd rather eat glass than apologize to that superficial, snooty tyrant, but he would. For Hannah, he would. ''Rent a billboard, hire a skywriter, write 'I'm sorry' in blood. You name it.''

Shaking her head, she got up and rummaged through her cupboard, then pulled out a crystal vase. ''I appreciate the offer, but you don't have to do anything. No one knows better than me how exasperating Aunt Martha can be. She'll forget about it soon enough.''

''You're not a very good liar, Hannah,'' he said evenly. ''That's not a criticism, just an observation.''

''So maybe she won't exactly *forget*.'' Hannah shrugged as she turned the water on to fill the vase in her hand. ''She's probably still gnashing her teeth over the 'heartless' comment.''

''God, Hannah. I'm sorry.'' He dragged a hand through his hair. ''I should never have said that—''

''It was wonderful.''

''What?''

''I said, it was wonderful.'' Clear plastic crackled as she pulled the wrapper off the flowers and dropped them in the water. ''You were wonderful.''

He stared at her, blinked. ''I was?''

She brought the flowers to the table and set them beside the pizza box, then sat back down again. ''No one has ever stood up for me like that before. Not since I was in the fifth grade and Tommy Belgarden punched Joey Winters in the nose for stealing my lunchbox.''

He reached out and took her hand, ran his thumb over her knuckles. "Good for Tommy."

She glanced down at their clasped hands. "She wasn't always like this," Hannah said quietly. "When I was a little girl, she'd visit my mother here and always bring me a present. I still have an Oriental wooden box with secret compartments that she gave me when I was seven."

Hannah smiled at the memory, then sighed. "I was eight when she married my uncle Lloyd and moved to Boston. She changed after that. She smiled less, rarely came to visit. After my mom died, she became fixated on me coming to live with her, and since my divorce and Uncle Lloyd's death she's become even more demanding. But I just can't move there. My life is here, in Ridgewater. It doesn't matter to me how hard I have to work, or how much I have to scrimp to get by. If I lose the house, then so be it. But I'm not leaving here."

He wanted to tell her that it would be all right, that she wasn't going to have to go anywhere, and she wasn't going to lose her house. A few well-placed phone calls to the right people this afternoon had made sure of that.

But after this morning, he doubted she would appreciate any more interference in her life. She didn't need to know about the phone calls he'd made, the favors he'd called in from different agencies. Sometimes it paid to be polite and knock on a door and wait for someone to open it. When you didn't have time to wait, you simply kicked the door down. He'd kicked several doors in today, because time was one thing that neither he nor Hannah had a lot of.

Her hand felt small in his, but he knew there was strength there. He'd never met any woman that he admired more, any woman who dazzled him the way Hannah did.

The thought, and the emotions it evoked, had him dropping her hand. He shoved the pizza box in front of her. "Eat."

Her blue eyes lit with pleasure as she took the first bite. She moaned softly. "I didn't realize how hungry I was."

His throat went dry as he watched her lick a spot of sauce from her lips. He hadn't realized how hungry he was either, but it wasn't for food. After the night they'd spent together, he couldn't just sit here and not want her, not want to touch her, kiss her, have her naked and writhing underneath him.

He took a slice of pizza instead, focused his appetite on food rather than Hannah.

"I'm sorry about asking you to leave earlier," she said after a moment. "I shouldn't have been so—"

"It's fine, Hannah. It gave me an opportunity to see the town, meet some people." He took a bite of pizza. "Did you know that June and Bob Chase are expecting their first baby, and that Charlie Thomas's truck was seen after ten o'clock parked in Mavis Goldbloom's driveway?"

"Everyone knows that June is expecting." Hannah's eyes sparkled with amusement. "And Charlie's the town plumber. Maybe Mavis had a plumbing emergency."

"That's what Perry Rellas said. Something about Mavis getting her pipes cleaned."

"Seth Granger, shame on you." She lifted a disapproving brow. "You're a gossipmonger."

He shrugged, plucked a pepperoni slice off his pizza

and popped it into his mouth. "Then I guess you don't want to know what I heard about Cindy Baker."

She paused, slid a curious glance at him, then lifted her chin and sniffed. "Certainly not. Cindy Baker is an acquaintance of mine. She was a cheerleader at my high school."

"Okay." He finished off his pizza slice and reached for another. "This is really good pizza."

"The best."

"Great crust."

"Fresh ingredients make a difference."

They ate silently for a moment, then she set her pizza down and frowned at him. "So are you going to tell me, or not?"

"What?"

She pursed her lips. "About Cindy."

"What happened to, 'shame on you for listening to gossip'?"

"Just tell me before I have to hurt you."

Grinning, he leaned forward and whispered, "She went to Dallas."

Sitting back in her chair, Hannah rolled her eyes. "That's it?"

"To get her pom-poms enlarged."

"Oh." She smiled. "That *is* a good one. And who told you that?"

"Billy Bishop."

"Billy Bishop?" She slapped a hand to her chest and stared wide-eyed at him. "You were fraternizing with Billy Bishop? The man you wanted to kill a few days ago?"

"Billy's all right." In spite of his irritation with Billy, Seth couldn't help but like the kid. All that youthful exuberance that hadn't been jaded yet by all the injustice and violence in the world. "We had a couple beers at the tavern and shot a few rounds of pool. I told him if he printed one more word about me, I'd have to break his arm, though."

"Well, you've certainly had a busy day." Shaking her head, Hannah reached out and wiped a smudge of pizza sauce on his mouth. He took hold of her wrist when she started to move away.

"Sorry," she said, blushing. "Habit."

"A nice habit." He brought her hand to his mouth, nibbled on the tips of her fingers. "Tasty."

He felt the shudder run up her arm to her fingertips, saw the glint of desire flare in her eyes. "You know that you and I are part of all that gossip now," she said quietly.

"Yeah." He paused, looked up at her. "Will that be a problem for you?"

Shivering, she leaned closer. "Nothing I can't handle. I haven't done anything I'm embarrassed about."

"Hmm." He turned her hand over, nipped at her palm, then tasted the hot, rapid pulse at her wrist. "Maybe we should work on that."

"Maybe we should," she whispered. "We have at least three hours before the girls get home."

"Three hours works." He stood, laced her fingers with his, then pulled her to him for a long, searing kiss. "For now," he murmured.

He led her to his bedroom, closed the door and made every minute count.

Ten

Seth had faced drug-crazed addicts, stared down the barrel of a loaded .357 and caught the tip of a butcher knife in his left shoulder. He'd been thrown fifteen feet from the blast of a meth-lab explosion, jumped through the second-story window of an apartment to dodge a bullet and been cornered by a pair of angry rottweilers.

What he'd never faced before, and had no idea how to handle, was a pair of stubborn five-year-olds.

Standing in the girls' bedroom, he held a tray with two steaming bowls of soup. Maddie and Missy sat under the covers in their bed, arms folded, bottom lips thrust out.

"We don't want soup," Maddie said.

"We want Charlie Choo Choo's Coco Crazies," Missy said.

Seth wasn't sure, but unless he missed his guess, Charlie Choo Choo's Coco Crazies was a breakfast cereal with a sugar content equaling a ten-pound Hershey's kiss. He might as well give them a bowl of M&M's and pour milk over them.

Not that he *personally* had a problem with that, but these were five-year-olds, after all.

"You're home from school because you're both sick." They'd woken up on their second morning back from camp with the sniffles and low-grade fevers. "Your mother left me in charge while she's working and told me to give you chicken noodle soup."

Maddie made a face and ducked under her covers. "We *hate* chicken noodle soup."

Missy slipped under the covers, too, and said from underneath, "It tastes yucky."

Terrific. They'd been at this already for five minutes and he'd made no headway in changing the girls' minds. "Maybe after your soup, you can have a small bowl of cereal," he coaxed, though he wasn't so sure Hannah would approve. He'd figured out enough in the short time he'd been here to know she carefully doled out sweets to her daughters, and only after they'd eaten a meal.

They both shook their heads, and Maddie said, "We want the cereal first."

"Then we'll eat some soup," Missy added.

Yeah. Like he'd fall for *that* one.

When Hannah had gotten the early-morning phone call from Phoebe asking her to cover a shift for one of the waitresses at the diner, Seth had offered to watch the girls. Hannah had refused at first, had told him that her daughters could be very difficult when they were sick. But he'd insisted he could manage just fine and she'd reluctantly agreed. Besides, he still owed her for the Aunt Martha debacle.

What could be so hard about watching a couple of little kids? he'd asked himself.

That was before the girls got out of bed every five minutes, wanting water, crackers, juice, napkins, a story, a game and to go outside and play. He'd cleaned up the crackers they'd used as Frisbees from one bed to the other, sopped up the spilled glass of water, then picked up the three thousand sparkling beads that had fallen out of the girls' jewelry-making kit. They grew crankier by the minute and an argument ensued when Missy took Maddie's doll and sat on it. He'd barely gotten them calmed down before it was time for lunch.

He was exhausted.

"Look, girls, I have to do what your mom says. Give me a break here and eat the soup."

"We don't *want* soup."

"We want Charlie Choo Choo's Coco Crazies."

"Maddie, Missy." He knew that he was pleading, that he sounded desperate. He didn't care. "One small bowl of soup, a few sips, maybe just a teeny, tiny taste. You can do that for me, can't you? Please?"

Maddie and Missy peeked out from under the covers. "Maybe," Missy said with a sniff. "But you have to have some soup, too."

That didn't sound so bad. No harm in having a little soup. "Okay."

"And we have to pretend the soup is tea," Maddie said.

Easy. "This soup is now officially tea."

The girls both smiled and jumped out of bed.

"Hey—" He watched them dash over to their bookcase and grab tiny cups and saucers and spoons. "You're supposed to stay in bed."

"We can't have a tea party in bed." Maddie rushed

over to the kid-sized table in the corner of the room and arranged a place setting.

Tea party? Now wait just a minute…

Missy pulled out one of the tiny chairs. "You sit here."

Oh, no. No no no no no *no*.

"No tea party." He shook his head. "I'm a guy. Guys don't do tea parties."

Nothing on earth could make him sit at a child's table and play tea party. Absolutely nothing.

Maddie's bottom lip started to quiver. Missy's eyes filled with moisture.

Seth set his teeth and gripped the tray tightly. He wouldn't cave. They could cry all they wanted, and he just didn't care. He refused to be manipulated by two five-year-olds.

And he absolutely, positively, refused to play tea party.

It didn't matter that her feet hurt and her arms ached from carrying heavy trays for the past six hours, Hannah practically skipped into the house when she returned home. She had a pocket full of fat tips, plus the hourly wage Phoebe had paid her. And while it didn't make much of a dent in her bills, every little bit helped.

The quiet that greeted her when she entered the house was a good sign. She hoped her daughters were napping. When they were sick and confined to bed, her little angels could quickly turn into little devils.

She headed for the stairs, paused at the top and listened. Based on the voices coming from their room, the girls were not asleep. With a sigh, she moved toward their bedroom, hesitated at the sound of Missy's voice.

"Would you like one lump or two?"

So they were playing tea party, were they? Which meant they weren't in bed. Shaking her head, Hannah was nearly at the doorway when the sound of Seth's deep voice stopped her.

"I'd like six, please."

Hannah peeked around the corner. Obviously too large for one of the tea table's chairs, Seth sat on the floor. Maddie sat on a chair beside him, sipping what smelled like soup from a tiny teacup, while Missy pulled a handful of Charlie Choo Choo's Coco Crazies from a box and counted out six.

Disbelief widened her eyes. Seth was actually playing tea party with her daughters!

Hannah ducked back around the corner before they could see her. She clapped a hand over her mouth so she wouldn't laugh at the sight of a six-foot-four, two-hundred-pound, rugged undercover cop from New Mexico sipping from a dainty teacup.

She listened to him compliment Missy on her excellent choice of tea, then suggest to Maddie that she have another cup. Carefully, Hannah peeked around the corner again, thinking that the tea did look suspiciously like soup. Smiling, she pulled back and leaned against the wall while she listened to the girls discuss where they wanted to have their upcoming birthday party, if they were going to invite boys, and what kind of cake they should have. When Seth suggested *fruit*cake, the girls broke into giggles and told him he was silly.

Something swelled in Hannah's chest. She closed her eyes, wished the intense feeling to be gone, but it only increased as she heard the silly banter between her daughters and Seth. The feeling moved up into her throat, swelled there, as well, then burned her eyes.

Damn you, Seth Granger, Hannah thought. *We were*

*doing fine before you came here. We were perfectly
happy and content, just the three of us.*

Hannah swiped at the tears sliding down her cheeks.

She'd fallen in love with him. Helplessly, hopelessly.
Completely.

The wrong man, at the wrong time, in the wrong
place.

The story of her life.

Quietly she crept back down the stairs, needing a
minute alone to compose herself, plus she figured that
Seth wouldn't be too happy about her seeing him sitting
on the floor with a teacup in his large, callused hand.
He might think it would seriously hinder his tough-guy
image that he worked so hard to maintain. He wouldn't
understand that it only made him all the more appealing.
More sexy, more virile, more desirable.

It frightened her how desperately she wanted this
man. Not only in her bed, but in her life. She didn't
understand how she could want that in such a short
period of time, but love didn't always fit neatly into a
formula. The fact was, she *did* want it. All of it. A ring,
the promise of forever. Babies. The thought made her
chest ache.

How she wanted to have Seth's babies.

Stupid, foolish thinking, she told herself as she
dropped her purse on the end table and headed for the
kitchen. Thinking that would only lead to heartache.

She'd bake a cake, she decided. A six-layer, double-
chocolate with raspberry filling. That would keep her
hands and mind occupied for a while.

Then later, she could eat half the damn cake herself.

That thought cheered her a little. She pulled ingredients out of her cupboard and refrigerator while she

hummed the latest Dixie Chicks' tune, poured oil into a measuring cup, then reached for an egg.

"You always were good in the kitchen."

Hannah whirled at the too-familiar deep voice behind her. The egg slipped from her hand and splattered on the floor.

"Brent."

He stood in the doorway, watching her, his hands in the pockets of his tailored tan slacks. He'd lightened his short brown hair with streaks of blond, and he'd either been to a tanning salon, or spending a lot of time lying around the pool at his town house. Probably both, she thought. She knew that most women fell for those blue eyes and flashing smile. She'd fallen herself once.

Now that she knew what was underneath those Ivy League looks, he only disgusted her.

Her ex-husband's gaze dropped to the floor, then slid back up to her face and his smile widened. "You're looking good, Hannah. Working at the diner?"

He nodded to the short-sleeved white blouse and black skirt uniform she had on. If she hadn't dropped the egg, she swore she would have thrown it at him just to see the expression on his smooth face when he messed up his white silk shirt. "What are you doing here?"

He frowned. "You could at least look a little happy to see me. Especially since I'm here with good news."

"You've relocated your business to Antarctica?" she asked, then decided she was being too nice. "Or maybe your current fiancée hasn't found out about the girl-friend you have in Fort Worth?"

He lifted a startled brow at that, clearly surprised that Hannah would know about it. "Have you been keeping tabs on me, sweetheart? Just say the word and I'll drop by to see you, too.''

The very thought made her ill, as did his endearment. She could have told him that Phoebe's cousin was general manager of the hotel where Brent always stayed when he travelled to Fort Worth, that he and a busty redhead rarely left the room when he was in town. But the fact was, she just didn't give a damn.

''You can call any time you want and see the girls,'' Hannah said evenly. ''If you've forgotten the number, I'll write it down.''

He shrugged. ''I've been busy. Maybe I'll come and see them at Christmas, take them to a movie or something.''

She'd heard that too many times to know he didn't mean it. He'd never call, and for that she was grateful. Turning, she grabbed for a paper towel and knelt to wipe up the egg she'd dropped. ''Just tell me why you're here, Brent. I'm busy.''

''I brought you a check.''

She narrowed a gaze at him, then dumped the egg mess in the sink and washed her hands. He'd never delivered a check in person to her, had never sent *any* money without at least three phone calls. ''Sure you did. And if I'm careful, I just might make it stretch into three, maybe four meals.''

''You wound me, Hannah.'' He pulled a folded piece of paper from his shirt pocket and waved it at her. ''It's right here. A cashier's check. Every penny.''

She hesitated, felt her heart miss a beat. Casually she turned, wiping her hands on a towel and stared at the piece of paper he waved at her as if she were a dog and he was teasing her with a meaty bone.

Her pulse started to race, but she refused to let him see any emotion from her. "What's going on?"

She saw something flash in his eyes, fear maybe? But it was gone just as quickly and the arrogance was back. He frowned at her, shook his head. "Didn't I tell you I'd pay you your share when the deal came through? Sweetheart, someday you'll learn to trust me."

When hell freezes over, she thought. Still, her curiosity got the better of her. She walked toward him and reached for the check. Grinning, he slipped it back into his pocket, then grabbed hold of her arm and pulled her close.

"Let go of me." Hannah twisted to get away, but Brent had never been a gentle man. His hand tightened painfully on her arm.

"Maybe you could be nice to me," he said, lowering his voice. "Show a little appreciation."

"Let me go," Hannah hissed through her teeth. "So help me, Brent, I'll—"

"Let her go."

Startled by the sound of another male's voice, Brent's head whipped around. His eyes widened at the size of the man standing two feet behind him. Instantly he released Hannah's arm.

"Who the hell are you?" Brent demanded.

Seth glanced at Hannah. He stood still, every muscle tensed, and she could feel the anger radiating from him.

"Are you all right?" he asked her, his voice quiet, controlled, yet laced with an undertone of fury.

"I'm fine," she said carefully, kept her gaze steady with his.

Seth nodded, then glanced back at Brent. "If you put your hands on Hannah again, you better have a good dentist and orthopedist. You got that?"

Brent paled under his tan, but managed to gather up enough courage to act indignant. "I don't know who you are, buddy, but if you think because you're shacking up with—"

Seth moved so quickly, Hannah didn't have time to stop it. Suddenly Brent's arm was bent behind his back and Seth was guiding him toward the front door.

"Wait!" Hannah cried out.

Seth stopped, looked back at her, his expression dark and his brow furrowed.

She ran to Brent, plucked the check from his pocket, then smiled at Seth as she opened the front door. "Okay."

Seth shoved the other man out the door and Hannah closed it. A moment later, they heard the sound of Brent's Porsche peeling rubber.

Hannah glanced at the check. It really *was* all there. Everything he'd owed her for the past three years!

Laughing, she threw herself in Seth's arms. He held her, but the tension in his body lingered. She rained kisses over his face, and slowly he began to relax.

"The jerk didn't even ask about his own kids." The word Seth uttered was crude.

"It doesn't matter," she said breathlessly. "He doesn't matter. Oh, Seth, this is so wonderful. Somehow a miracle occurred and he actually paid me. I won't lose the house. I can pay my bills. I can open the Wild Rose. It's everything I ever wanted."

But even as Seth pulled her closer and kissed her long and hard—a kiss that surely would have ended in the bedroom except for two little girls upstairs—even as she kissed him back, she knew it was a lie.

Everything had changed since Seth had shown up. Everything she'd thought she'd ever wanted and everything that she'd thought would be enough, suddenly wasn't.

She pulled away from him, smiled through the tears blurring her vision. "I'm going to go check on the girls now. Then I'm going to come back down and bake you the biggest chocolate cake you've ever seen."

"A man can't hardly argue with that." He grinned at her. "What kind of wine goes with chocolate cake?"

Smiling, Hannah tipped her head and said in a high-pitched whine, "Maddie's piece is bigger than my piece."

It took him a beat to catch her joke, then he groaned and dragged her close for another kiss. "Hannah Michaels, you are one hell of a woman."

His words warmed her, made the longing rear up in her chest again. Her knees were weak as she made her way up the stairs, her heart heavy. But for the moment, for this tiny space in time, she was happier than she'd ever been in her entire life.

The Fruitcake Festival had begun.

The people of Ridgewater, and neighboring towns as well, turned out in droves for the annual event held on the Ridgewater High School football field. Food and game booths lined the outer running track and a country-and-western band played on the forty-yard line. The scent of barbecued chicken and hamburgers filled the warm September air while the sounds of a Clint Black tune beckoned young and old alike to clap their hands and strut their stuff.

And in the midst of it all, enclosed in a clear plastic display case which sat on an American-flag-draped grandstand, was the World's Largest Fruitcake.

Four feet tall, six feet round, one hundred pounds of

fruit and fifty pounds of nuts, the humongous glossy dark cake sat proudly on the center-field line.

"She's a beaut, ain't she?"

Seth glanced at the short, balding man who'd stepped up beside him. Charlie Thomas, the plumber. Seth wasn't certain if Charlie was talking about Hannah, who stood under the grandstand speaking to Lori's husband, or if he was talking about the fruitcake.

Seth glanced back at Hannah. She was laughing at something John had said. "Absolutely stunning," Seth murmured.

When she looked over at him at that moment and smiled, Seth felt his gut tighten. He knew Charlie was rattling off statistics about the fruitcake, but the words simply weren't registering.

She'd bought a new dress: soft lilac, long and flowing with a scoop neck and tiny white buttons marching up the front. When she'd walked down the stairs this morning, a blush on her pretty cheeks, she'd made him ache. He'd wondered, if only for a moment, what it would be like to watch her walk down those stairs every morning, what it would be like to fall asleep in that big bed of hers every night, to wake up with her in his arms.

They never made love when Maddie and Missy were home, were careful not even to touch except for an occasional stolen caress or kiss. But when the girls were at school, when Hannah wasn't out covering a shift at the diner or running her endless errands, they'd reach for each other, breathless and eager. This past week had gone by quickly. He'd surprised her by setting the tile for her in the upstairs bathroom, a skill he'd picked up from one of his dozen jobs between high school and joining the force. He'd also painted the upstairs bedroom she'd been working on, replaced the broken fence slats in the front yard and repaired a leaking faucet off the back patio.

He'd forgotten how good it felt to work with his hands. To repair something, then stand back and be satisfied with a job well done. How long had it been since he'd felt a sense of accomplishment or pride, since he'd felt that what he did or who he was mattered? Since he'd felt that he belonged, really belonged?

His adopted parents had been good to him, they'd loved him in their own quiet way, but something had always been missing. Seth looked around, saw the energy of the people surrounding him, the happy, excited faces. This was all so familiar, yet not familiar at all.

He watched two young boys run by with cotton candy and felt the ground shift underneath him. Heard an odd buzzing in his head, then voices, almost as if someone had just flipped on a movie...

"...and the first-place winner of the nine- and ten-year-old division of Junior Bronco Rodeo is Rand Blackhawk, son of Jonathan and Norah Blackhawk of Blackhawk Ranch." Pride swelled in Seth's chest as his big brother stepped forward and the man pinned a shiny blue ribbon on his chest. *"Look, Mom, look, Dad, it's Rand,"* he said pointing. *"He won! He won! Rand won!"*

Seth looked up at his mother's smiling face, her bright eyes and wavy brown hair. She held Lizzie on one hip, two years old only three days earlier, and his sister's big blue eyes were wide with excitement at all the commotion surrounding her. Rand raced down the steps and joined his family, turned bright red when Kristen McDougall, a pretty blonde in the fifth grade ran up and hugged him, then ran away.

They threw darts at balloons, tossed dimes onto

smooth glass plates, ate hot dogs with catsup and pink, soft clouds of cotton candy...

"...and requires an oven big enough to drive a Buick into," Charlie was saying. Seth stared at the man, saw his mouth moving, but barely made out the words. The image of that day more than twenty years ago stayed with Seth, made his hand shake and his chest tighten.

His mother.

His father.

Rand. Lizzie.

He'd dreamed of his family over the years, but the dreams were always fuzzy. He'd remembered bits and pieces of his life when he was small, but there'd never been anything concrete, certainly never anything as clear, as strong or as detailed as the memory that had just jumped into his head.

He didn't remember anything about the night of the accident, the night he'd lost his family. But he knew that Seth Blackhawk had died that night, too. He'd been reborn Seth Granger. A new home, new parents, new school.

And it had never *felt* right.

Never.

He shook the feeling off, forced himself to listen to Charlie. Somehow—though he didn't understand how—Seth was certain that whatever the man was saying, it was important.

"...my granddaddy laid the foundation and Andy Philpot's granddaddy set the bricks," Charlie said. "'Course, that was nearly eighty years ago now, and the oven was a woodburner back in those days. Not easy to keep her at an even 275 degrees for three days, but everyone pitched in shoveling wood until Henry Willard's daddy brought in gas pipes...'"

"Seth!" Maddie and Missy came running up, their blue eyes bright and cheeks flushed. "Come see, come see. They're gonna cut the cake now!"

"Apologize to Mr. Thomas for interrupting," Hannah said as she came up behind her daughters.

"Sorry," both girls said together, then each grabbed one of Seth's hands and pulled. "Come on!"

Seth looked at Hannah. "You mean they actually eat this monstrosity?"

"Of course we eat it." Hands locked behind her back, she followed along beside Seth and her daughters. "What did you think we did with it?"

"What everyone does with fruitcake." He let himself be pulled into the growing crowd. "Wrap it back up and send it on to the next person, who wraps it up and sends it to the next person, and so on. Word has it, there's just one lonely fruitcake that circles the world. 'Course, with this puppy—" he looked at the giant cake "—you'd need a freighter to ship it anywhere."

Hannah rolled her eyes at his nonsense, then turned her attention to Mayor Mooney's official cake-cutting speech, a rousing tribute to Wilhems' Bakery, tradition and community spirit.

The mayor raised a silver, foot-long knife, held it over his head like a sword, then applause and whistles broke out from the crowd as he placed a slice of cake on a silver plate. "This year's honorary first slice is presented to—" the mayor paused dramatically, then glanced at Seth.

Oh, God, no…

"Seth Granger!"

He narrowed a gaze at Hannah, who appeared to be as startled as he was. Maddie and Missy jumped up and down, then Seth found himself pulled up on stage. Too stunned to resist, he faced the mayor, was forced to listen to a highly embellished recap of his bravery over saving Maddie, then accepted the slice of cake the mayor placed in his hands.

The crowd went quiet, stared intently at him, and Seth realized that three thousand people were all waiting for him to take a bite. Teeth set, he scooped up a chunk and popped it in his mouth.

Dense, but moist. Molasses-sweet, with a light crunch of nuts and a faint taste of fruit.

Damn. It tasted *good.*

When he raised his fork, the crowd cheered. When Billy Bishop snapped a picture, Seth frowned darkly.

Everyone received a slice after that, and the festival proceeded with a Garth Brooks number from the band and a magic act on the grandstand. Seth endured the hand-shaking and back-slapping from the townspeople while Hannah danced a two-step with Wilson Jones, the elderly man who owned the tavern in town. When a younger, good-looking guy took the next dance and slipped his arm around Hannah's waist, Seth moved in quickly and stole her away.

She's mine, Seth said silently as he smiled at the disappointed man. *All mine.*

The day went by quickly. They ate hot dogs with catsup, threw darts at balloons, tossed dimes on smooth, glass plates and ate cotton candy.

"Just concentrate on the sight." Seth moved behind Hannah at the Ducky Decoy Rifle Shoot, leaned down close so their bodies touched. "Aim high and squeeze the trigger slowly."

She wiggled to get in position, and the innocent brush of her bottom against his groin sent instant fire through his veins.

Squinting at the yellow metal duck that moved across blue wooden waves, Hannah took aim and fired. And missed. "I'm not very good at this," she said with a frown.

"That depends on where you're standing." He waggled his brows when she slid a glance at him over her shoulder.

A blush rose on her cheeks. "You're distracting me."

"I was thinking the same thing." He leaned closer and whispered in her ear, "You smell like cotton candy. Did I ever tell you how much I like cotton candy?"

"Too much sugar will rot your teeth," she insisted, but he felt her move into him, saw her blue eyes darken with desire.

"Life is full of danger," he murmured. "Sometimes you just have to—"

"Hey, Seth! I been looking all over for ya!"

Both Seth and Hannah pulled away at the loud, deep voice. It was Ned, from the repair shop.

Dammit, anyway.

With a sigh, Seth straightened, looked up and shook the mechanic's extended hand. Ned was six-foot-eight, a huge barrel-chested biker with a meticulously trimmed moustache. Ed, his son, stood beside him. At nineteen, Ed was only six-five, the runt of the litter, so Ned had told Seth when they'd met in town last week.

"Hey, Hannah." Ed stared moon-eyed at Hannah. When she smiled back, the kid turned bright red.

"Got good news for you." Ned handed Seth a key. "Finished your bike two days early. Ed rode it over here on a test drive and she screams like a bi—"

Ned glanced at Hannah, caught himself before he finished the crass remark about to come out of his mouth.

"Ah...she runs great. Anyway, your insurance took care of the bill, so she's all yours."

Seth stared at the key in his hand, then looked up at Hannah. The blush that had been on her cheeks only a moment before had faded, the light in her eyes gone.

"Thanks." Seth slipped the key into the front pocket of his jeans, felt the metal burn through denim and scorch his skin. "Thanks for everything."

"Nice to see you Ned, Ed," Hannah said with a smile that didn't make it to her eyes. "But you'll have to excuse me. Lori took the girls to the face-painting booth ages ago and I better go check up on them."

When Seth moved to go with her, her smile widened, but a look of near panic lit her eyes. "You stay," she insisted. "Talk shop. I'll be back in a little while."

She hurried away, and Seth started to go after her, then stopped. What good would it do? What would he say? They'd never talked about it, but they'd both known he'd be leaving when his motorcycle was repaired.

He didn't have a clue how to say goodbye. To Hannah or the girls. But he knew he needed to.

When he turned back to Ned and Ed they discussed the new air-cooled engines *vs.* the water-cooled, debated the question of whether a bike could have too much chrome, but Seth's mind wasn't on the conversation. It was on a pretty blonde in a lilac dress and two little five-year-olds who loved Charlie Choo Choo's Coco Crazies.

Hannah rolled the window down on the drive home from the festival, let the first crisp chill of autumn waft through her car. In a few days, pumpkins and straw scarecrows would decorate porches and storefronts, and shortly after that, the scent of cinnamon and apples and roasting turkeys would fill the air.

She'd always loved this time of year. The fun and excitement of sewing Halloween costumes, the blessings of Thanksgiving dinner, then the joy and chaos of decorating a Christmas tree and wrapping presents. The Fruitcake Festival had always signalled the start of the holidays, was the first ripple of anticipation of the upcoming weeks.

But tonight was different from all the others. Tonight she felt no excitement, no joy or thrill of anticipation.

Tonight would be the last night she'd spend with Seth.

She pulled into her driveway, saw him sitting on his motorcycle in front of her house and felt her heart slam against her ribs.

Since Ned had handed Seth the key to his bike, there'd been no opportunity to discuss when he'd be leaving. But she knew. She'd seen it in his eyes after he'd slipped the key into his pocket, felt it in her heart. He'd be leaving in the morning, she was certain.

She wouldn't ask. She'd known all along that he'd leave when his motorcycle was repaired. There'd been no promises, no plans for the future. He had a life in New Mexico, a job, and her life was here.

Arms loaded with two stuffed teddy bears, a purple armadillo and an orange parrot, she slid out of her front seat and headed toward her front door.

"Where are the girls?" He met her at the porch steps, took the stuffed animals from her, then waited while she dug through her purse for her house keys.

"They're having a Mickey Mouse movie marathon and sleepover at Lori's." The smile she forced felt tight and thin, but it was the best she could do.

Normally she wouldn't let them stay over after such a busy day, but she'd made an exception tonight. She knew it was selfish, but tonight she wanted Seth to herself.

Hannah opened the door and stepped into the house, closed the door behind them when Seth followed.

They stood in the entry in the dark and faced each other. The silence wrapped around them like a heavy fist. Neither one of them moved.

"Hannah," he said quietly. "I—"

"Don't." She reached out, touched his lips with her fingertips, then leaned forward and replaced her fingers with her lips and whispered, "Don't say it, Seth."

The stuffed animals fell to the floor. His arms came around her so quickly, so tightly, she gasped. His mouth covered hers, tilted her head back in a fierce, hungry kiss that left her breathless and weak. She kissed him back, made love to him with her mouth and her body. With her heart.

He'd take that with him when he left, she thought. Her heart, her love.

She was young, maybe she'd love again someday, but not with such depth. Maybe another man would spur her to passion, but not with this intensity. There would never be another Seth. She would never feel this way again, of that she was absolutely certain.

She wound her arms tightly around his neck, pressed closer to him, heard the soft moan rise from deep in her throat. The urgency had them both breathing hard, moving toward the bedroom as one. Her sweater slipped off near the base of the stairs, his shirt at the bedroom door. Between eager, hot kisses, clothes slipped away until they both fell naked and breathless onto his bed.

She felt the chill of cold air on her breasts, then the

heat of his mouth. He tasted and teased, nipped at her soft flesh until she was gasping and weak with need.

Together they rolled, arms and legs entwined, bodies joined. She rose over him, felt the rhythm, moved with it. His hands dug roughly into her hips, held tight as they spiralled upward with the rising passion. She arched back, felt the need for release claw at her.

She took him with her, to the edge, hovered there, then tumbled over. With a deep, low moan, he followed.

"Hannah," he said raggedly, then dragged her mouth to his. His arms wrapping around her, they rolled to their sides and faced each other, waited for the breath to come back to them and the ground to stop spinning.

Her heart still pounded in her chest as she touched his cheek. He turned his face into her hand, pressed his lips to her palm.

"I rushed you," she whispered. "I'm sorry."

He laughed softly. "We've got time yet."

Not enough, she thought. Not nearly enough. But she wouldn't think about that now. She couldn't.

Moonlight sliced through the shadows and stretched across their bare bodies. Hannah inched back, rose on her elbow and rested her head on her palm while she took in the sight of him. The hard planes of his face, the broad expanse of his chest, the long, solid stretch of leg. Every angle, every feature, she committed to memory.

"There's something I need to know." She traced the square line of his jaw from earlobe to chin, felt the rasp of his evening beard on her fingertip. "I need the truth."

"I wouldn't lie to you, Hannah."

He hadn't before, she knew. He'd always been honest, about everything. "The check that Brent suddenly showed up here with? Did you make that happen?"

"Hannah, I—"

"The truth, Seth. Please."

He shifted awkwardly beside her. "I'm sorry, I know you told me to stay out of—"

She kissed him to shut him up. "Thank you."

He lifted a brow. "You aren't mad?"

Smiling, she shook her head. "Of course not. It took me a couple of days to figure it out, though I still can't imagine how you made it happen."

"I made a phone call or two," he said with a shrug. "It was suggested to him, by certain people in high places, that unless he wanted every state, city and county inspector blocking every project he was involved in, and every project he'd ever be involved in, then he needed to clear up some back financial matters."

"You could do that?" She blinked at the moisture burning her eyes.

"It was no big deal." He wiped at a tear that slid down her cheek, frowned. "Hey, don't. Don't cry."

"I'm not," she lied. "Not really. I'm just…grateful, that's all."

For so many things, she wanted to tell him. No matter what the pain, she was glad he'd come into her life, so very glad.

They were quiet for another long moment, then she said, "Seth, I think it's better if I say goodbye to the girls for you. They might not…understand."

I don't understand, she wanted to say. When he sighed, then pulled her close, she clung to him, let the fever sweep her away and make her forget, if only for the moment, that in the morning he would be gone.

Eleven

A miniature railroad display sat in the corner of Henry Barnes's oak-paneled office. Seth stared at the elaborate creation, a depiction of a mountain coal-mining town, complete with general store, hotel and saloon. The train itself, a shiny black replica of an 1800s locomotive, was meticulous in detail, from the brass-plated bell and whistle on the engine, to the forest-green watchtower on the caboose.

The display made him think of the dollhouse in Maddie and Missy's bedroom. The girls had spent hours with their tiny plastic people and furniture, arranging and rearranging all the hundreds of tiny little pieces that drove Hannah crazy. If she wasn't stepping on them, she was sucking them up in the vacuum cleaner. He smiled at the image of Hannah, hands on her hips, lecturing the girls on responsibilities and taking care of their toys.

His smile slowly faded. He'd been gone less than two days, but it felt longer. He'd left before dawn yesterday, kissed her on the cheek while she was still sleeping. Afraid if she'd woken up, he wouldn't have left.

But they'd said their goodbyes the night before. Made love, talked about the girls, the festival, his motorcycle. They talked about everything but his leaving, had both wanted it that way.

Hadn't they?

A phone ringing from the outside office caught his attention, and he turned his attention back to the railroad display. Inside the general store, a thumb-sized male clerk wearing an apron stood behind a counter where tiny shelves were lined with canned goods and folded squares of blue-checkered linens. Realistic trees and shrubbery surrounded the tunnel leading into the mountain where tiny workmen shoveled coal into hopper cars.

Seth looked at the switch that turned the train on and felt his fingers twitch, wondered if the engine blew smoke like the one he'd had as a kid. He'd been six the Christmas his father had brought home a train layout and set it up under the tree. He could still smell the crisp scent of pine, see the jeweled glass ornaments and sparkling white lights, hear the sound of his mother's holiday music playing.

He and Rand had played for hours under that tree, arguing over who got to be the engineer. The smile on his face faded as he realized that in a short while, after twenty-three years, he and his brother would stand face-to-face. Eye-to-eye.

Seth shoved his hands into the front pocket of his jeans, not only to resist touching the controls of the train, but because his palms were suddenly damp.

"Sorry to keep you waiting." Henry Barnes came into the office, glanced up from a file folder and smiled. "Victoria Wellington, the president of the horticulture club, was insistent on filing a lawsuit against Ernie Farson's new puppy for digging up Vickie's prizewinning dahlias. It took me a few minutes to convince her that there were other ways to handle the problem than litigation."

The gray-haired lawyer wore a charcoal sport coat over a white-collared shirt, blue dress jeans and shiny black cowboy boots. When he saw that Seth was inspecting his train setup, the older man's dark-brown eyes brightened.

"Just got her set up last week. Keeps me out of trouble and the grandkids love it. Henry Barnes." He held out a hand. "Just call me Henry."

Henry's handshake was firm and sincere, eased the knot in Seth's stomach. Henry moved around his large oak desk, gestured for Seth to sit in a leather armchair opposite him.

Henry leaned back in his chair, a thoughtful expression on his face as he stared at Seth. "Damn if you two don't look alike," he said, shaking his head. "This has got to be the damnedest case I've ever had."

Impatience gnawed at Seth's gut. "I thought my brother was going to be here."

"We agreed it might be best for me to explain a few things to you first." Henry sat forward and opened the file he'd brought in with him. "Get the basics out of the way."

The sudden stab of disappointment surprised Seth, but he merely shrugged. "All right."

"Everything is in here." Henry turned the file around and slid it across the desk to Seth. "Dates, times, names. We can go over all the details now, or I can give you the shortened version and you can take this file with you.''

Seth glanced at the file. There were several pages, in small print. ''Let's go with the shorter version.''

''I thought that's what you'd say.'' Smiling, Henry pushed a button on his desk intercom. ''Judy, can we get two cups of coffee in here? And hold all my calls, please.''

Henry flipped the intercom off and settled back in his chair. ''Why don't you get comfortable, Seth? Even with the shortened version, this might take a while.''

Two hours later, Seth stood at the window of his fifth-story Four Winds Hotel room and stared at the town below. Across the street, a man walked out of the drugstore, the same drugstore where Seth's mother had bought him red licorice when he was a kid. A barber pole three stores down still turned in swirls of red, white and blue, the same barbershop where his father had taken him for a haircut. On the corner, a yellow neon sign flashed from the glass window of a diner. The same diner where he'd sat in a booth with his family and eaten hamburgers and chocolate shakes.

As he'd driven through town, more memories from his childhood came back to him. It wasn't that he remembered names or faces as much as he remembered the smells and the sounds. The scent of fresh-baked bread from the bakery, the smooth, rich taste of strawberry ice cream in a wafer cone from the drug store, the deep, hollow bong of the church bell every Sunday at noon.

Dammit. He squeezed his eyes shut, wanted desperately to remember more, to remember what had happened that night. He knew what Henry Barnes had told him, of course. But it was just so hard to believe.

Shaking his head, he turned away from the window and stared at the file sitting on the corner table. It was all there, the proof, and it was *still* so damn hard to believe.

He opened the file, stared at the copy of the newspaper clipping inside, read it for the tenth time...

Family Of Five Killed In Storm-Related Accident Jonathan and Norah Blackhawk, long-time residents of Wolf River, and their three children, Rand, age nine, Seth, seven, and Elizabeth, two, were killed late Saturday night when their car spun out of control in Cold Springs Canyon...

Every time he read that part, every time he saw their names in print, a shiver crept up his spine. The article went on to describe the lightning storm, how the medics had pronounced them all dead at the scene, that they were survived by William Blackhawk, Jonathan's brother.

Every time Seth read the name *William Blackhawk,* he saw red. William Blackhawk, his own uncle, his father's brother, had orchestrated the deception. Henry Barnes had explained to Seth that William had hated both of his brothers, Jonathan and Thomas, for marrying outside of the reservation. William had shunned both brothers and their children, even though they'd all lived in Wolf River.

Seth didn't remember his uncle, couldn't understand how a grown man could turn his back on his own family, go to the lengths that he had to falsify the deaths of three children, then cruelly send each of them out for adoption, telling each child individually that the rest of their family was dead.

But he did understand, Seth thought with disgust and tossed the article back into the folder. Greed motivated most crimes, Seth had certainly learned that in his job. Greed and passion. William had been consumed with both. Greed for the land and money—a *great* deal of money, it turned out—that Seth's grandfather had left in his will to his three sons. And his passion had been his hatred toward his brothers' Anglo wives and their half-breed children.

If his uncle hadn't died in a plane crash two years ago, Seth thought he might kill the man himself.

With a sigh, he stared at the folder, then closed it. He'd memorized everything in there he needed to know.

Spencer Radick, the town sheriff and first person on the accident scene, who had called William. The sheriff left town two months later and hadn't been seen since.

Rosemary Owens, William's housekeeper, who had taken Rand that night and kept him until he was adopted by a family in San Antonio. Rosemary had left Wolf River six weeks later and moved to Vermont, and they now knew she died of lung cancer only six months ago.

Leon Waters, a crooked lawyer from Granite Springs, who arranged all the illegal adoptions and forged death certificates. Seth didn't remember him, but Henry had told him that Waters was also the person who had taken him from the accident scene, then made arrangements with the Grangers to adopt him immediately. Leon had closed up his practice shortly after the accident and disappeared.

Their participation and silence had all been bought and paid for by William Blackhawk. The deception might never have been discovered if not for a journal

found after Rosemary's death, a thorough documenta-
tion—names, places, dates—everything that took place
that horrible night and the days following. The journal
had been sent to the only Blackhawk still living in Wolf
River, Lucas Blackhawk, a cousin Seth never knew he'd
had. He owned a ranch just outside of town, was married and had two children.

And there was another cousin, Seth had learned. William had a son, Dillon Blackhawk. But Dillon had left
Wolf River when he was seventeen and had never returned, not even for his father's funeral. Considering
who his father was and what he'd done to the Blackhawk family, Seth didn't much give a damn where William's son had gone, or if he ever came back. What did
a person say to the man whose father had lied and
ripped a family apart?

There were still scores to settle, men to find, justice
to be served. But that would be dealt with later.

The only thing that mattered to Seth now was Rand
and Lizzie. Though they were still looking for Lizzie,
Rand had returned to Wolf River, Henry had told him,
and was planning to settle down here with his fiancée.

Seth glanced at the phone. He knew that his brother
was waiting for a call. Seth had walked over and picked
up the receiver at least half a dozen times, then put it
back down.

He didn't have a handle on his emotions just yet. His
head was still spinning from everything he'd learned
this morning at the lawyer's office. He'd call in a little
while, he told himself, as soon as he felt in control.

He paced back to the window, watched a wavy-haired
blonde step out of the drugstore across the street,
thought for one heart-stopping moment that it was Han-

nah. It wasn't, of course, and he shook his head at his foolishness.

She'd be picking up the girls from school about now. He could picture them pulling into the driveway. If Mrs. Peterson was in her front yard, she'd wave while Beau barked a greeting. Then the girls would run into the house for a snack and Hannah would ask them about their day. They'd both talk at once, maybe Missy had won a game of handball or Maddie had painted a picture that she wanted to be hung on the refrigerator, or maybe they'd give an update on Derek Matthews's most recent antics in the classroom or on the playground.

He rubbed at his chest, felt an ache there. He missed them. God, he missed them.

Turning away from the window, he stared at the phone again.

No. He shook his head. If he called her it would only make it more difficult between them. Complicate their relationship even further. Hannah deserved more than he could ever offer her and the girls. Even now, Jarris was waiting for him to get back to New Mexico, had told him that his next assignment would be long-term and high-risk. In the past, Seth had asked for exactly those types of jobs, had looked forward to them.

"Dammit."

He dragged a hand through his hair and headed for the door. There was a bar downstairs. He'd have a beer, something to eat, then he'd call Rand.

With his mind still on Hannah, Seth opened the door, froze at the sight of the man standing in the hallway.

It was almost like looking in a mirror, he thought, too stunned to move. The reflection in front of him was the same height, same build, though the other man wore a denim long-sleeved shirt and Seth wore a navy-blue

T-shirt. They both wore jeans, had the same dark eyes and black hair, though Seth's was longer.

Neither man moved, both stared intently at the other, muscles tensed, breaths held.

"Rand?" Seth's voice was barely a whisper.

"Hey, Seth."

A knot formed in Seth's gut as he looked at his brother. Twenty-three years fell away. He was no longer standing in a hotel room, he and Rand were in a ravine, lying on their bellies behind a fortress of rocks...

"I'm wounded, Sergeant Blackhawk," Rand said in *his biggest grown-up voice. "Do you understand what your assignment is?"*

"Yes, sir, Captain." Seth saluted. "To infiltrate en-emy lines and bring back reinforcements, sir." They both knew that "enemy lines" meant their mother's kitchen, and "reinforcements" were the chocolate chip cookies she'd baked that morning.

"Don't let me down, Sergeant." Rand gasped, as if he were taking a dying breath. "I may not last long out here, and the troops are counting on you to save us all..."

The memory, no more than a blip on a radar screen, disappeared. Seth blinked, stared at his brother.

The knot in Seth's gut turned into a lump in his throat. His heart, which he swore had stopped beating, started to bang in his chest.

"Damn," was the only word that he seemed capable of saying.

Rand grinned. "Yeah."

In the next second, two strong men, brothers found, grabbed on to each other and slapped each other's backs.

Though neither one would ever admit it, they both

had to blink back the moisture in their eyes when they parted.

Seth struggled to hold on to his emotions. "I was just going to call you."

"Yeah, well, I was in the neighborhood." Then he shrugged. "I'm not the most patient guy."

"Mom used to say you had the patience of a corn-crib rat."

They both smiled at the silly saying as much as the shared memory.

"Never quite knew what that meant," Rand said, shaking his head.

"Me, either."

"I heard you're a cop."

"I heard you're working with horses."

There was a lot to catch up on, they both knew. So much to talk about.

A lifetime.

"You know about Lizzie?" Rand asked.

"Just what Henry told me. That you've hired a private investigator named Jacob Carver to find her."

Rand nodded. "Shouldn't take too long to locate her. The people who adopted her were living out of the country at the time, but we think they've moved somewhere on the east coast."

"She won't remember us." He thought of his sister's big blue eyes, her bright smile and infectious laugh. "She might not even want to remember us."

"It's a chance we'll take," Rand said. "Whatever she does, we have to accept and respect her decision, but at least she'll know the truth. She deserves that much. We all deserve that."

Rand placed a hand on Seth's shoulder and grinned.

"You up to a trip out to the ranch while we catch up? Check out the old homestead?"

Seth's pulse quickened at the thought. Would his and Rand's old bedroom still have blue walls? Would the screened wooden back door still squeak when it opened and closed? Would the marbles he'd hidden under a floorboard in the hall closet still be there?

It would be fun to find out, he thought, and grinned back at Rand. The house had been a simple one, he remembered, the rooms small, but his mother, his father, Rand and Lizzie, they'd all made it a home.

His life may have changed after the night his parents had died, but there were things that always stayed the same, the memories, the feelings. Even after twenty-three years, Seth knew that Rand was still his brother, not just in blood, but in spirit. Nothing could ever change that, or what they'd shared as children. And though he was certain that Lizzie wouldn't remember him or Rand, he still hoped that somehow she might feel that bond.

Seth ate dinner at his cousin Lucas's house that night, met his wife, Julianna and Rand's fiancée, Grace. They all sat around a big table. Nathan and Nicole, Lucas's three-year-old twins, blessed the food and thanked God for their new baby brother, two-week-old Robert Jonathan. They toasted Seth, then passed roast beef and mashed potatoes. The conversation never lagged. The questions were endless, the answers fascinating. It felt like family, felt like home. Felt like he belonged.

And still there was something missing.

Something didn't feel right. Something that went beyond Lizzie not being a part of the celebration.

He knew that no matter how far he ran, or how much

he lied to himself, it was something that couldn't be denied.

He was scooping up a bite of apple pie, listening to Grace describe how Rand had single-handedly rescued a small band of horses trapped in a canyon, laughing at the embarrassment on Rand's face, when it struck him like a two-by-four in the solar plexus.

He knew at that moment exactly what was missing. Knew exactly what didn't feel right.

What he didn't know, what he hadn't figured out yet, was what he was going to do about it.

The pounding beat of Donna Summer's disco music vibrated off the walls and shook the dining-room chandelier while fifteen little girls and boys marched around fourteen folding chairs set up in the middle of Hannah's living room. Lori's husband, John, directed traffic, kept the children moving around the chairs until the music stopped. Then all fifteen children screamed at once and dived for the nearest empty seat.

"You want me to scoop ice cream now?" Lori yelled over the din of excited children.

"Wait until the game is over," Hannah yelled back. "I've got a table set up outside and we'll serve everything out back. Why don't you go help John?"

They'd already sung "Happy Birthday" and blown out candles and Hannah had sent the party guests off to play a game while she sliced the cakes—chocolate with chocolate frosting for Maddie, and white with pink frosting for Missy.

The girls had changed their minds at least a dozen times over the past week, couldn't agree whether to have a party at the bowling alley, the miniature golf course, the park or the pizza parlor. But in the end, they'd both decided they wanted to have a Betty Ballerina party at their own house, with a sleepover for all the girls in their class. After the week they'd all had since Seth had left, Hannah would have let the girls invite the entire school, the entire town, if it would make them happy.

Her daughters had cried a week ago when they'd come home from Lori's and he'd been gone. Hannah had explained as best she could. He had family he had to go see, a job he needed to get back to in New Mexico.

Hannah had saved her tears for the night, after the girls had gone to bed.

The only thing that had cheered the girls up, and Hannah, too, had been planning this party. They'd shopped for decorations and balloons, made invitations, made lists of games to play and bought prizes. And aside from party preparations, Hannah had taken on extra hours at the diner, cleaned out her flower beds and set out fall colors in mums and marigolds, stripped the wallpaper in the corner upstairs bedroom and bought fabric to sew curtains for the downstairs bathroom.

She'd welcomed the exhaustion that came at the end of every day. What other way to help heal a broken heart than to keep hands and mind busy?

The music stopped again, the laughter and screams vibrated through the house, then the groans of the children who'd been left standing.

That was how her life felt right now, Hannah thought as she filled the paper plates with cake. As if she'd been walking in circles, then the music had stopped and there was no place to sit.

"Everybody outside!" Hannah heard John yell when the game ended. "Who wants first swing at the piñata?"

Fifteen children screamed *me!* and tore out the back door like stampeding cattle. Determined to have a good time, Hannah grabbed a Betty Ballerina party tiara and stuck it on top of her head. She went into the kitchen and retrieved the ice cream out of the freezer, grabbed an ice-cream scoop from the drawer and walked back into the dining room.

She heard the *whack!* of the baseball bat against the pumpkin-shaped piñata John had brought over and set up, then the excited screams of the children. She wouldn't mind taking a couple of whacks at the thing herself, she thought. Maybe it would ease a little of the tension she'd been carrying around in her neck and shoulders all week.

"Something I can help you with?"

She froze at the sound of his voice, then turned slowly, breath held.

Seth.

He stood in the dining-room entry. Clean-shaven, dressed in a black buttoned-up shirt, blue jeans and black cowboy boots. He leaned against the doorjamb, arms folded casually, a crooked smile on his lips. "Nice tiara."

She slipped the party hat from her head while her heart slammed against her ribs. It took every ounce of willpower she possessed not to run at him, to throw herself in his arms and kiss every inch of that handsome, wonderful face.

If it weren't for Maddie and Missy, she would do that. She'd make a fool out of herself, beg him to stay. But her daughters deserved better than that. *She* deserved better than that, Hannah thought. She didn't want him for a day or a week. She wanted him forever, dammit. Nothing less.

She felt the anger flicker deep inside her, hadn't even realized that it was there, that it had been there all week, brewing underneath the surface. If the girls saw him now, got their hopes up, it would be twice as hard next time he left.

She turned back to the ice cream, scooped up a ball of vanilla. "Why are you here, Seth?"

He pushed away from the doorjamb, made her stomach lurch when he took a step toward her. "I wanted to tell you about my family."

He'd come all the way back here just to tell her about his family? Stopping by on his way back to New Mexico to chat with her before he moved on again?

Well, she didn't want to know about his family. She didn't want to know what had happened, or what he'd been doing. She wanted him gone. Out of her life.

Liar, liar, liar.

All right, so she *did* want to know, she admitted to herself. She desperately wanted to know everything, every minute, every detail.

But she kept her voice calm, her hand steady as she dropped ice cream on a plate, then scooped up another ball. "Did it go well?"

"Very well." He took another step closer. "My brother is remodeling the house where we grew up. He's getting married next month and asked me to be his best man."

"Oh, Seth." In spite of the ache in her heart, Hannah smiled. "That's wonderful."

"You'd like Grace, Rand's fiancée." Seth eyed the cakes on the table. "And Julianna, too, my cousin's wife."

"You have a cousin in Wolf River?"

"Lucas Blackhawk. He's got three-year-old twins, Nathan and Nicole, and a two-week-old little boy."

Weddings and babies and family reunions. Hannah didn't think she could take much more of his good news without breaking into tears.

From outside, she heard the children laughing and the heavy pounding of the baseball bat on the piñata. She had ice cream to scoop, dammit. Cake to serve. Presents still to be opened.

She couldn't fall apart now. She *wouldn't*.

"I'm happy for you, Seth. Really, I am." She practically flung the ice cream onto the plates. "I appreciate you coming by, but I think it's best if the girls don't see you. Now, if you'll excuse me, I've got to get back to the party."

He stepped closer, looked hopefully at the table. "That cake sure looks good."

"Seth." She closed her eyes, sighed. "Why are you here?"

"I left something."

She'd been through the entire house, had secretly hoped that he had left something. She'd found nothing. "What did you leave?"

"You."

She went still at his single word.

You.

Her heart pounded furiously. When she didn't move, didn't look at him, he slipped the ice-cream scoop from her hand and set it on a plate, then took hold of her shoulders and turned her to face him.

"I left you behind," he said quietly. "You and Maddie and Missy."

"What are you saying?" She still refused to let herself hope, afraid—terrified—that the music might stop and she'd be left standing.

"I've missed you this past week." His gaze held steady with hers. "I found a brother, a cousin, an entire family, but it still didn't feel right. My life still felt as if there was a hole, an empty space."

"Seth." She gripped the fabric of his shirt in her hands, heard the impatience in her own voice. "*What* are you saying?"

"I'm saying—" Seth paused, hadn't known that he was capable of the feelings he had, the intensity and the depth "—I'm saying that I love you."

"You—you love me?" she whispered.

"Yes." He smiled, tugged her close and brushed her lips with his. "I love you. And I love Maddie and Missy, too. I'm saying that I want you to marry me."

Her head came up on a soft gasp. "You want me to...*marry* you?"

He'd had days to think about this, hours and hours of carefully rehearsed proposals, then every word had been forgotten the moment he'd seen her standing in the dining room, wearing that silly party hat and scooping ice cream onto paper plates.

"I want you to marry me." He touched her cheek with his fingertips, smiled at the look of complete bewilderment on her face. "Will you?"

"But you—" she shook her head "—but what about, I mean, you can't—"

He kissed her, as much to give himself a moment as for her. He dragged her close, deepened the kiss until she melted against him and made a soft little sound in her throat.

"Tell me you love me, too, Hannah," he murmured against her lips.

"Of course I love you." She laid her palm on his cheek. "I've loved you from that first day you came crashing into my life. *Our* lives," she corrected herself.

"Will you have me?" he asked. "You and Maddie and Missy?"

"But your job—"

"I quit my job. The only undercover work I want from now on is with you, in our bed." He gave her a quick peck on the lips. "Besides, I can get a job here. Ned and Ed are looking for a mechanic, you know."

She narrowed a gaze at him. "You're teasing me."

"Only about the job. I was hoping you might teach me how to run a bed-and-breakfast." He decided he'd tell her about the five million dollars he'd inherited later. Over a midnight bottle of champagne they could figure out together what to do with all that money. "Now hurry up and say yes before I explode."

"Yes." Breathless, she wrapped her arms around him. "Yes, yes. I'll marry you."

He pulled her close, covered her mouth with his and poured himself into the kiss, all his love, his need. They broke apart at the sound of a loud thump, then the shrill earsplitting screams of fifteen children scrambling for candy.

He touched her forehead with his, waited for his heart to settle back into a steady pace. "I can't wait for you to meet my family. They can't wait to meet you."

She looked up at him in surprise. "You told them about me?"

"Why wouldn't I tell them about the woman I love, the woman I'm going to marry?" He took her chin in his hand. "As soon as we set a date for the wedding, I'll call my mom in Florida, too. She's always wanted me to have a big wedding. How about the weekend before Thanksgiving?''

''Thanksgiving! But that's—'' Hannah counted in her head ''—three weeks from now!''

''You're right, that's too long,'' he said, narrowing his eyes. ''Let's make it two weeks from today.''

Laughing, she threw her arms around his neck. ''I can't plan a big wedding that quickly. I'll need a dress, flowers, the reception, invitations would have to go out.''

''We'll call Billy Bishop,'' Seth said. ''He can print our invitation on the front page of the *Ridgewater Gazette*.''

Hannah's eyes widened. ''You want to invite the *entire* town?''

''Absolutely. I even want to invite Aunt Martha, if she'll come.''

''She'll come.'' Hannah smiled up at him. ''Can you believe she sent me flowers this week, and she actually apologized for her behavior?''

He lifted both brows. ''Are we talking about the same aunt?''

''The only aunt I have. You're a miracle worker, Seth Granger.''

''Actually—'' he met her gaze with his ''—I'm going to change my name back to Blackhawk. It's something I need to do, Hannah. I hope it's all right with you.''

''Mrs. Seth Blackhawk.'' She touched his cheek. ''I love it. I love you.''

He kissed her again, a tender, gentle press of lips, a promise of forever.

Eyes bright with moisture, Hannah tilted her head up and looked at him. ''So it won't bother you to live here,

in Ridgewater?" she asked. "Home of the world's largest fruitcake?"

"I'd have to be the world's largest ass to let that
bother me," he said with a grin. "My home, my life,
is wherever you are, Hannah. You and the girls."

As if on cue, Maddie and Missy came running into
the house, asking where the cake was. When they saw
Seth, they both shrieked and ran at him. He scooped
them up, kissed each flushed cheek.

"We blew out the candles and wished you'd come
back and you did!" Maddie said.

"We got our wish!" Missy threw her arms around
Seth's neck.

Smiling, he leaned toward Hannah. She met him half-
way. "Me, too." He touched his lips to hers. "Me,
too."

*   *   *   *   *

Lizzie's story is coming soon.
But first, don't miss
Barbara McCauley's
contribution to Silhouette's

CROWN & GLORY

series—available in December
from Silhouette Desire.

Silhouette *Desire*

presents

DYNASTIES: THE CONNELLYS

A brand-new miniseries about the Connellys of Chicago,
a wealthy, powerful American family tied by blood to the
royal family of the island kingdom of Altaria.
They're wealthy, powerful and rocked by
scandal, betrayal…and passion!

Look for a whole year of glamorous and
utterly romantic tales in 2002:

January: **TALL, DARK & ROYAL by Leanne Banks**

February: **MATERNALLY YOURS by Kathie DeNosky**

March: **THE SHEIKH TAKES A BRIDE by Caroline Cross**

April: **THE SEAL'S SURRENDER by Maureen Child**

May: **PLAIN JANE & DOCTOR DAD by Kate Little**

June: **AND THE WINNER GETS…MARRIED! by Metsy Hingle**

July: **THE ROYAL & THE RUNAWAY BRIDE by Kathryn Jensen**

August: **HIS E-MAIL ORDER WIFE by Kristi Gold**

September: **THE SECRET BABY BOND by Cindy Gerard**

October: **CINDERELLA'S CONVENIENT HUSBAND
by Katherine Garbera**

November: **EXPECTING…AND IN DANGER by Eileen Wilks**

December: **CHEROKEE MARRIAGE DARE
by Sheri WhiteFeather**

Silhouette

Where love comes alive™

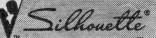

Three bold, irresistible men.
Three brand-new romances by today's top authors...
Summer never seemed hotter!

Sheiks of Summer

*Available in August
at your favorite
retail outlet!*

"The Sheik's Virgin" by Susan Mallery

He was the brazen stranger who chaperoned innocent, beautiful
Phoebe Carson around his native land. But what would Phoebe do when
she discovered her suitor was none other than Prince Nasri Mazin—
and he had seduction on his mind?

"Sheikh of Ice" by Alexandra Sellers

She came in search of adventure—and discovered passion in the arms
of tall, dark and handsome Hadi al Hajar. But once Kate Drummond
succumbed to Hadi's powerful touch, would she succeed in
taming his hard heart?

"Kismet" by Fiona Brand

A star-crossed love affair and a stormy night combined to bring
Laine Abernathy into Sheik Xavier Kalil Al Jahir's world. Now, as she
took cover in her rugged rescuer's home, Lily wondered if it was her
destiny to fall in love with the mesmerizing sheik....

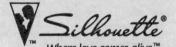

Silhouette®
Where love comes alive™

Beloved author
JOAN ELLIOTT PICKART
introduces the next generation of MacAllisters in

The Baby Bet:
MacALLISTER'S GIFTS

with the following heartwarming romances:

On sale July 2002

THE ROYAL MacALLISTER
Silhouette Special Edition #1477
As the MacAllisters prepare for a royal wedding,
Alice "Trip" MacAllister meets her own Prince Charming.

On sale September 2002

PLAIN JANE MacALLISTER
Silhouette Desire #1462
A secret child stirs up trouble—and long-buried
passions—for Emily MacAllister when she is reunited
with her son's father, Dr. Mark Maxwell.

And look for the next exciting installment of
the MacAllister family saga, coming only to
Silhouette Special Edition in December 2002.

*Don't miss these unforgettable romances...
available at your favorite retail outlet.*

Silhouette®
™
Where love comes alive™

COMING NEXT MONTH

#1453 BECKETT'S CINDERELLA—Dixie Browning
Man of the Month/Beckett's Fortune
Experience had taught Liza Chandler not to trust handsome men with money. Then unbelievably sexy Beckett Jones strolled into her life and set her pulse racing. Liza couldn't deny that he seemed to be winning the battle for her body, but would he also win her heart?

#1454 HIS E-MAIL ORDER WIFE—Kristi Gold
Dynasties: The Connellys
Tycoon Drew Connelly was unprepared for the sizzling attraction between him and Kristina Simmons, the curvaceous bride his daughter and grandmother had picked for him from an Internet site. Though he didn't intend to marry her, his efforts to persuade Kristina of that fact backfired. But her warmth and beauty tempted him, and soon he found himself yearning to claim her....

#1455 FALLING FOR THE ENEMY—Shawna Delacorte
Paige Bradford thought millionaire Bryce Lexington was responsible for her father's misfortune, and she vowed to prove it—by infiltrating his company. But she didn't expect that her sworn enemy's intoxicating kisses would make her dizzy with desire. Was Bryce really a ruthless shark, or was he the sexy and honorable man she'd been searching for all her life?

#1456 MILLIONAIRE COP & MOM-TO-BE—Charlotte Hughes
When wealthy cop Neil Logan discovered that beautiful Katie Jones was alone and pregnant, he proposed a marriage of convenience. But make-believe romance soon turned to real passion, and Neil found himself falling for his lovely bride. Somehow, he had to show Katie that he could love, honor and cherish her—forever!

#1457 COWBOY BOSS—Kathie DeNosky
Cowboy Cooper Adams was furious when an elderly matchmaker hired Faith Broderick as his housekeeper without his permission—and then stranded them on his remote ranch. Cooper didn't have time for romance, yet he had to admit that lovely Faith aroused primitive stirrings, and promoting her from employee to wife would be far too easy to do....

#1458 DESPERADO DAD—Linda Conrad
A good man was proving hard to find for Randi Cullen. Then FBI agent Manuel Sanchez appeared and turned her world upside down. He proposed a marriage of convenience so he could keep his cover, and Randi happily accepted. But Randi was tired of being a virgin, so she had to find a way to convince Manuel that she truly wanted to be his wife—in *every* way!

SDCNM0702